JOIN THE CREATIVE PROCESS.

VOTE

for the cover you like best!

We value your experience and keen eye.
Be part of the creative collaboration at

www.thelmabee.com

Win an exclusive Thelma Bee gift box with peculiar swag,
perfect to turn any office, library, or bookstore into a
Riverfish Valley Paranormal Society (RVPS) meeting place
for ghost hunters and book enthusiasts alike!

Deadline to Enter: August 1, 2016

Check back for updates, reviews,
awards, and more!

The PECULIAR HAUNTING of Thelma Bee

BY
Erin Petti

WITH ILLUSTRATIONS BY
Kris Aro McLeod

mighty media JUNIOR READERS

MINNEAPOLIS, MINNESOTA

Meet the Peculiar Crew!

Alexander   Thelma

Eugene   Mr. Understone

Izzy

The Scientific Method:
Middle School Hazards

(OBSERVED)

Thelma Bee dragged still-sleepy fingers through her bangs as she marched into the backyard. October was serving up another perfect day—chilly air, crispy leaves, and early sun. She knelt down to pat the New England soil with a careful hand, trying not to disturb the small green plant cutting, then grabbed the notebook from her back pocket and scribbled,

Day 4. Control specimen—no sign of growth.

Stretching her arms up to the sky, Thelma breathed in deep and exhaled with a little shoulder shake. She crossed her backyard to the second vanilla orchid. This was the experimental one. As she approached, she opened her duffle bag, took out a small sombrero and placed it on her head, and then pulled out her breakfast burrito.

"*Buenos días poco orquídea* vanilla," she said with aplomb.

The scientific method dictates that one must start with a question:

QUESTION: Can cultural or outside forces have an effect on how a living thing grows?

HYPOTHESIS: A flower that is native to Mexico can grow right here in Riverfish, Massachusetts, if you surround it with elements from its natural habitat.

Thelma had wheedled Mr. Chen into giving her two small vine cuttings from his greenhouse, even though she suspected he didn't have much faith in the efficacy of her experiment.

Steadfast for days, Thelma had eaten only Mexican food, spoken only Spanish, and even played mariachi music around the plant. As she chewed a mouthful of delicious *salchicha*, Thelma noted that despite her efforts, there wasn't much growth to report. She wiped off the grease around her mouth with her sweater sleeve and grabbed her pen. Under Day 4, she added:

Experimental specimen—no sign of growth. But expectations remain HIGH!

She underlined the last bit twice.

Experimentation, exploration, it was in Thelma's blood. At that very moment, in fact, her mom was backpacking the Smoky Mountains, investigating reports of a humongous elk-like animal she'd affectionately nicknamed "Mega-deer."

Thelma often dreamt of the day when she would adventure through the world like her mom, Mary Bee. Uncovering nature's mysteries and making important discoveries in the wild—what could be better? Also, possibly winning a Nobel Prize, getting rich, and making certain fellow sixth-graders (ahem, Jenny Sullivan, ahem) super jealous.

Wiping her dirty hands on her jeans, Thelma straightened up and surveyed the yard. It seemed like only yesterday that she and her dad were spending warm evenings around the fire pit, setting up tents, and spying muskrats in the bushes. Now, instead of green, it was all wild yellows and reds. Some trees had already lost their leaves. Thelma's yard abutted the Beaverbottom River, and the chilly water made a low rushing sound as it flowed past.

Thelma watched the water and touched the small opal that hung around her neck on a delicate silver string, a birthday gift from Mom. She'd told Thelma that the opal was sometimes called a rainbow stone or a lightning stone, because of the way it could look plain one minute and flash incredible colors the next. Thelma didn't like jewelry usually. It had the annoying habit of getting caught up on things, and it made trying on scuba gear a huge pain. But this necklace was special because it reminded her of Mom, so Thelma pretty much never took it off.

The quiet morning, cool soil, slow river, and crisp air gave Thelma an infinity feeling. Like everything was connected to everything else. Like anything was possible.

But then in a disappointing turn of events, her big blue wristwatch beeped three times. If she didn't start walking to school soon, she'd miss the bell.

"Hey!" Alexander shouted down the crowded hallway.

This year, Thelma and Alexander only saw each other twice during the school day—during Mr. LeBouf's drama class and at lunch. As they were currently in the middle of a pantomime unit, Thelma and Alexander weren't allowed to talk during drama, so lunch was basically their only time to hang out. After years of being in the same class, this middle school schedule stank.

"Thelma, wait up!" Alexander yelled, pushing his shaggy black hair out of his face.

Thelma stopped and waved her arm over her head. Finally, it was time for food and some decent company. Also, she had to catch Alexander up on the latest information. Most urgently, the vanilla orchid's progress … or lack thereof. He'd have some valuable input for sure.

"Thelma, your boyfriend is calling for you!"

Ugh. Thelma felt a sick pit in her stomach. That was the unmistakable, nasally voice of Jenny Sullivan. She was flanked by her friends, or as they would describe themselves, "Besties." This particular friend designation was etched onto matching bracelets each girl wore. Thelma pondered whether the bracelets contained GPS or other tracking systems so they could find each other when they got lost at the mall.

Jenny Sullivan had started plucking her eyebrows this year, and it gave her a severe and unnatural look, like a Kabuki mask. On this particular day she wore a T-shirt that read, "I hate math homework" in a loopy font meant to appear girly. Thelma looked away, bit her lip, and tried not to gag.

Jenny waved her hands in front of Thelma's face. They smelled like corn chips.

"Hello! Um, I'm talking to you!"

"Your hands smell like corn chips."

"Yours do, freak!" Jenny snarled.

"No," Thelma said, sighing in exhaustion, "The corn chip smell is definitely coming from your hands. You actually have some stuck in your braces. Right in the middle, there."

"Whatever, weirdo." Jenny

snapped. Her eyes veered to the right, a clear sign that she was searching her brain's left hemisphere for some kind of comeback. Then she put her hand up to her mouth, irrefutable evidence that she was trying to find chip residue in her braces.

"Nice necklace, Thelma. It looks like you stole it off a ... like, an old lady," said Aisha Garr, a pug-nosed brunette who wore clip-on earrings because her mom wouldn't let her get her ears pierced—a source of deep shame for some reason.

Jenny smiled and clarified Aisha's statement, "It's lame. Your necklace is lame."

Thelma bit the inside of her lip. Despite herself, she felt a lump in her throat. Jenny was just being her normal jerky self, but when she made fun of Thelma's necklace, it felt like she was making fun of Mom.

"We think you're the weirdest," Amber Biddle piped in, her over-glossed lips pursed in a superior expression.

"Yeah," echoed Jenny, "why don't you try to *Bee* normal, Thelma *BEE*? Get it?"

Again, they laughed.

Thelma felt her temperature rise. Something uncontrollable happened when she felt angry or uncomfortable or embarrassed. Her whole body filled up with heat, and her normally pale complexion turned all shades of scarlet. Blushing quadrupled the embarrassment. More embarrassed, more red-faced. More red-faced, more embarrassed.

Thelma clenched her teeth and tried a trick her dad had taught her. First, breathe. Then, in your head, count backwards from ten, nice and slow. *10 Mississippi, 9 Mississippi, 8 …*

Thelma opened her eyes slowly once she heard the retreating sound of the girls' dumb bracelets clattering like jingle bells. It was like Santa's whole sleigh was taking off.

Alexander jogged to catch up with Thelma as the gang strutted away, all eye rolls and mean giggles.

"They really think they're comic geniuses, don't they?" he asked with his brow knit in genuine befuddlement.

Thelma exhaled, touching her necklace, "Yeah, whatever. She stinks like chips. Anyway … no luck with the orchid yet."

"Oh, man!" He removed his glasses to wipe them on his sleeve, and Thelma could see pale imprints on the bridge of his nose where the glasses dug into his light brown skin. "Have you been consistent with the morning routine?"

"Of course I have!"

"Well, there's more time for observation, right?"

Alexander played an instrumental role in the Mexican vanilla orchid experiment. He'd even made some homemade salsa (extra spicy) for one particularly delicious after-school snack in the yard.

"Yeah, totally. Presentation's not for another week."

"Maybe you could get an extension if there's no

growth by then? I still have a good feeling about this, but we can't rush things," a thoughtful scowl crept across his face.

Thelma nodded. "I'm starving," she said, adjusting her heavy backpack. As usual, her locker was jammed, so she lugged all six of her textbooks around. She imagined her spine turning into an S-shape under the constant burden.

The two parted ways as they entered the cafeteria. Alexander always brought lunch and Thelma always forgot to take the lunch that her dad left on the counter for her. She liked most of the cafeteria food, though. Especially pizza.

Thelma moved eagerly through the lunch line with visions of melted cheese dancing in her head. She was the kind of hungry where if you visualized eating food, you actually began to salivate. A very cool trick of the nervous system, she thought, mouth watering in anticipation.

It was probably worth some research—just how does the brain do that to the mouth? Thelma reached back into her backpack at an awkward angle and grabbed her notebook, almost bumping a huge hockey jersey that seemed to be wearing a seventh grader. Close call.

She found the "Future Experiments" list and scribbled:

QUESTION: Could you trick someone into enjoying a bowl of kale if you bombarded

them with images of a crispy crust, tangy
fresh tomato sauce, yummy cheese?

Thelma's stomach growled loudly, and she shoved her pen back into her pocket.

When Thelma was just a few feet away from the lunch lady, a smell hit her square in the olfactory nerve. The odor was heavy, greasy, fried, oily—her stomach churned with sudden nausea. Tater tots.

There was no way—no way in the whole universe—that she was eating tots. Or, for that matter, food that had been living next door to tots all morning, soaking in their disgusting odor.

It was bad enough that she had to lug around these heavy books all day, and it was bad enough that she had to put up with Jenny Sullivan's garbage-stinking attitude and her dumb shirt, but now no lunch? No pizza? It was too much. Thelma's pulse quickened in anger. She huffed and fumed over to the wobbly cafeteria table where Alexander meticulously unpacked his salad.

How could Riverfish Public Schools think that it was appropriate to serve fried, grease-drippy, potato puffs to their students? Their starving students! She clenched her fists and her cheeks began to feel hot.

Filled with tater tot rage, Thelma swung her six-book-heavy backpack down on the rickety cafeteria table. It made a huge, gratifying noise on impact. But then it happened.

What occurred next was, as any scientist would admit, a true study in cause and effect. Thelma would have considered it a fascinating series of events if it weren't a complete disaster, and entirely her fault.

It went like this:

1. Thelma slams down backpack on poorly constructed cafeteria table.

2. Cafeteria table lurches like a seesaw, causing a Styrofoam bowl of tomato soup to jump off the surface and onto the floor, creating a large red puddle.

3. Juddy McDougal, not known for ballerina-like grace, steps into large puddle of tomato soup. His body slips and slides in an objectively hilarious fashion before falling on his backside.

4. Juddy's best friend Ernesto, having observed this feat while eating a Ziploc bag of grapes laughs so hard that a grape chunk gets caught in his windpipe, and he begins to choke.

5. Mrs. Borfinger, the cafeteria lady in charge of the operating the frialator, sees Ernesto wrapping his hands around his neck in the international sign for "I'm choking!" and she rushes from behind the counter to his rescue. Borfinger successfully administers the Heimlich maneuver on Ernesto.

6. In Borfinger's absence, however, a grease ball in the frialator ignites and becomes a mass of flame and smoke.

7. Principal Tork runs across the cafeteria in the style of an Olympic hurdler, jumping over a table of seventh graders as if he were on track for an international record. He rips off his blue button-down shirt with one pull and tries to bat down the fire. When unsuccessful, he finds the fire extinguisher and blasts the frialator with a storm of white foam.

8. The entire cafeteria sits in shocked amazement at their shirtless principal, covered in foam, standing triumphantly over the burned-out frialator.

Alexander pursed his lips and grabbed Thelma's arm. "Just have some of my salad, OK?" he said.

Frog-Eating Visitor

(UNSUBSTANTIATED)

To Thelma's relief, the rest of the afternoon passed without further life-or-death drama. The clock struck 2:30 P.M., and Thelma burst out of the school, carving a path through the weird-smelling ocean of middle-schoolers. When she made her way to a clearing, she set a course for her dad's antique shop.

Thelma's dad, Henry Bee, was the proud owner of Bee's Very Unusual Antiques. The name of the store was a little bit of false advertising, of course. Sometimes they sold items that were ordinary, like an old chipped mug, and sometimes they sold things that were not antique at all, like Mrs. Edelstein's home-made cookies. The shop should probably be named something more like Bee's Very Unusual Antiques and Also Some Very Normal Antiques and Also Cookies.

"Hey, Dad!" Thelma threw down her backpack and plopped on an overstuffed chair. The soft embrace of the cushions was an incredible relief after a long day. She hoped her dad wouldn't ask how school was, because then she'd have to tell him about the cafeteria incident. It's one thing to stretch the truth when you're talking to a teacher or store clerk who wants to know why an eleven-year-old needs to buy grappling hooks (how else was she supposed to scale the town hall?) but she had never been able to lie to her dad.

"Hey, kid!" Dad yelled. He'd obviously been hard at work. He emerged from the workshop looking happy and disheveled. He wore a worn-out apron and had a smudge of yellow paint on his cheek. It reminded Thelma of the David Bowie poster they'd just gotten in stock.

"Thel!" said Henry, "I got something to wreck."

"Yeah?" Her ears perked up, "Like, wreck wreck?"

"Total destruction," said Dad. He motioned toward a ratty old loveseat in the middle of the floor. "We've got to really tear it to shreds. I want to keep the bones, but that's it."

"Destruction day!" Thelma hopped up and lunged to grab the multi-toothed fabric-ripper her father held out to her. Building was great—she loved building. But some days, some especially tater tot-ish days begged for the sweet release of totally annihilating a tacky loveseat. Henry laughed.

Thelma didn't need any instruction. She turned

the radio up loud and began ripping stuffing out of the seat, tear-
ing without precision, stripping it
down to its skeleton. She was lost
in a reverie of wailing guitars, flying cotton, and shredded burlap
when she noticed a figure in the
doorway.

The lady was small and hunched. She
had a thick pile of silvery white hair
on her head, a twitchy nose, and a
large mark on her neck that was visible from twenty feet away. The mark
demanded attention on the papery neck
of the old lady. It resembled a bull's head—two
horns pointing up toward her little chin.

Thelma tried not to be rude and stare, but
it was hard to look away. The mark was dark
and purple against the lady's pale skin. It almost
looked like some kind of tattoo. But an old lady
with a neck tattoo? That would be extremely
peculiar. Thelma considered the possibilities:

A. The lady belonged to some kind of indige-
nous tribe.

B. She was a competitive wrestler in a previous career.

C. She was a competitive wrestler
now—"Grammy Tammy the Tat-
tooed Tackler."

Thelma imagined this little old lady in a leotard holding a beefy muscleman in a choke hold.

That ridiculous image made Thelma want to laugh, but the impulse faded when she looked back up at the woman's form. She was hunched, but not under the burden of age or old bones. She looked coiled like a snake. Poised. Ready for something.

"Hello!" Henry greeted, turning down the radio. He brushed couch stuffing off his pants. "Can I help you, ma'am?"

"I saw your sign in the window," she said. "You take ... ehm, you buy old pieces?" The lady's voice was the sound of tires on a gravely drive.

"Yes, indeed," Henry smiled broadly.

The old lady carried a package. It was small and wrapped in brown paper like Thelma's textbooks.

She thrust the package forward with surprising force in her arms. "I'd like to sell this to you."

"Sure, OK! Let's take a look." Dad led the woman over to a wide, wooden table, pushing aside the folds of purple fuzzy fabric that lay there. As he slid his fingers gently under the paper wrapping, the lady cleared the gravel in her throat. It was the kind of throat-clearing noise characters on TV make before they say something important. The two Bees stared at her expectantly, but she just stiffened and frowned even deeper than she'd been frowning before, which was quite an achievement.

"Frog in my throat." Her nose twitched. And a bull

on your neck, Thelma thought but didn't say out loud. Actually, the old lady did have the face of a frog-eater.

Thelma put down her fabric ripper and ambled over to the worktable to see what was inside the mystery package. It was always exciting when folks came to sell items to Dad, especially when unwrapping was involved.

The little lady fiddled with her long unpolished nails and they made a clicking-clacking sound. There were more than a few layers of brown paper to peel through. It was kind of awkward, the two of them hovering over her dad while he carefully unfolded the paper, and Thelma wasn't good with long silences.

"So ..." she searched for a mutually interesting topic, "Are you going to the Applekin Festival this weekend? People have been talking about the gourd contest this year and it sounds like there are going to be some amazing—"

"No. I won't be going," the lady snapped. "I'm not from this area." Her eyes darted from Thelma's face to the table.

"Oh. Where are you from?" Thelma asked.

"Elsewhere."

That was the end of that conversation. Grumpy for an old lady, thought Thelma. Not that she wanted to stereotype old ladies, but most of the ones she knew were pretty nice. For instance, it would be hard to picture any of them eating live frogs. This one was a different story.

"My, my, my ..." Dad sounded amazed as he removed his glasses and put his face close to the freshly revealed jewelry box. It was made of a light, old wood with a maple-and-cherry veneer. There were two tiny brass knobs on the box, shaped like interlocked hands. He was transfixed, examining the piece inch by inch.

The lady looked pleased. "I'd like to sell it. Today, please. Right now would be best," she said.

A dog barked outside and the woman jolted.

"That's just Tuna," Thelma said. "Captain Axelrod's dog. She's nice, but birds drive her bananas."

Henry Bee put his thick glasses back on.

"Absolutely. We'd love to buy this from you," he said. "This is a nice piece—local, I think, right? And very old ..."

The lady dropped her chin in a curt nod.

"Yeah," continued Henry, "I don't know if we have anything like this here."

"You don't." The lady said the words in hiss so quiet that Dad didn't hear her. Thelma did, though. The old lady exhaled sharply and glanced at Thelma, who trembled a little.

"I'm sorry," Dad continued. "We've been so rude! My name is Henry Bee, and this is my daughter, Thelma Bee." He stuck out his arm for a handshake.

"Good. Cash would be best for me. That is, if you have it. And I expect you do."

"Right." He raised his eyebrows and withdrew his

unshaken hand. Thelma had very little patience with people who acted disrespectfully towards her dad. She quietly fumed.

"OK, then," said Dad, "Well, what were you thinking, in terms of price?"

"It's rare, you said so yourself. Two hundred dollars." The lady's nose twitched again, like she had a fickle sneeze stuck up there.

"All right. Well, if that's your price, I'll have to make another appointment with you. I just made a big purchase this morning," he gestured to the old loveseat they'd been ripping apart, "so I've only got about a hundred or so in the store right now. But two hundred is fair for this, I think, so ..."

"One hundred is fine. That's fine."

Dad paused, and cocked his head a little. "Are you sure? I'm willing to pay you the full price ..."

"I said one hundred is fine. Only a fool would try to negotiate the price up, Mr. Bee. Are you a fool?" The old lady's pointy words snapped like a mousetrap.

OK, Thelma thought, even an itchy nose could not excuse that kind of rudeness. *10 Mississippi, 9 Mississippi, 8 Mississippi....* By the time she got to 3, Henry and the lady were already mid-transaction.

"Let me take you into the office. We'll get you a receipt and make this official." He led the twitchy visitor away with a polite smile.

Thelma peered over at the shop's new treasure. She got a funny twisting feeling inside. Something between a stomachache and the nasty sensation she had gotten the time she wore a boys' flannel shirt to school and Jenny Sullivan made a huge deal of it in front of everyone. I mean, who even knew that girls' shirts button on the left and boys' on the right? Who knew and who would possibly care? Besides, of course, Jenny Sullivan: Jerk Police.

Thelma tried to swat the sick feeling away as she ran her hands over the box with curious fingers. She lifted it up, and it wasn't heavy at all, which surprised her. Grabbing one of the brass knobs, she pulled. It was stuck. She pulled harder and harder, but still nothing. After a few minutes of searching for a secret lever, she gave up.

Thelma turned back to the loveseat to resume the destruction project. The old lady and her weirdo box had taken some of the wind out of her sails, but Thelma was determined to continue enjoying her work.

She squared her shoulders and repositioned herself, ready to take an excellent whack at the armrest when there was a crash. The jewelry box had fallen off the table. It was loud. Really loud. Had Thelma done that somehow? Her mouth twisted into a scared grimace. A hundred dollars was so much allowance to save. And she had other plans for her allowance money, big plans. Plans that involved a waterproof telescope, scuba gear, and a trip to Lake Winnemusket.

She listened carefully for a moment to see if the conversation in her dad's office had been interrupted.

Had they heard the crash? But then she heard the lilting of Dad's friendly voice, and she knew she was safe.

Thelma bit her thumbnail nervously. With all the stealth she could manage, she crept back across the workshop floor toward the toppled jewelry box. It looked OK, thank goodness. She bent down and grabbed both sides to lift it back up to the table, but something was odd. It felt different. It felt really heavy.

It sounded like they were finishing up in her dad's office, so Thelma quickly bent her knees and, with a great deal of effort, hoisted the thing back up onto the table. Very curious, she thought.

Glancing down at her watch, Thelma realized it was almost time for her meeting with Alexander. This mysterious antique had made her lose track of time and now she only had five minutes to get to Barney Beans. Tardiness was not an option.

A further inspection of the jewelry box confirmed no damage, so Thelma wiped her forehead, exhaled in relief, and exited out to the front of the store. She looked back and saw the old lady and her father shaking hands. They'd made a deal.

Ghost Facts

(ACCORDING TO E)

Thelma walked down Riverfish's tree-lined street, taking in the autumn scenery on her way to Barney Beans. Town Hall was decked out in blinky lights in preparation for the Applekin Festival, which was positively the most exciting town event of the year. It was even better than February's Snow-a-Palooza and July's Blueberry Bazaar, which was really saying something.

Each year during the festival, the third-graders from Riverfish Elementary reenacted the town's historic founding. It was always hilarious, even though it wasn't supposed to be a comedy. Thelma's favorite character was the giant talking bear. Legend had it that a magical bear led brave Reverend Thickthorp and his aptly named wife, Patience, to the banks of the Beaverbottom back in the early

1700s. Usually the adults in charge of the reenactment put two kids in a giant bear suit, one for the front half, one for the back half of the costume.

Three beeps on the big blue wristwatch reminded Thelma to hurry up or she'd be late to the meeting. Her notebook had an entire page devoted to new invention ideas. Alexander was crazy about inventions. Personally, she wished they would spend their meeting time talking about new strategies to get to the top of Town Hall so she could finally get cracking on creating her hand-drawn map of Riverfish. But this was an invention meeting—and Alexander was right, it was totally important to keep new ideas flowing—that way you never run out. She strolled down to Barney Beans and reviewed a checklist:

☐ A bookmark that saves your place at the exact line (with a light for night reading)

☐ Cough syrup that tastes like real cherries and not fake medicine cherries

☐ A school elevator that operates both vertically and horizontally, because stairs are really only half the transportation battle

The door jingled as Thelma entered Barney Beans. Immediately the warm scents of chocolate, chai, and fresh coffee greeted her.

The café's original owners, Bernardo (Barney) and Eugenia, were an older couple who now lived down in Sarasota, Florida, where the manatee watching was top notch. In Bernardo and Eugenia's absence, their son Eugene ran the show. Eugene was a wide-smiling, skinny young guy who always put tasty free samples of the Torte del Dia on the counter for folks to munch on. He was in the middle of steaming some especially volcanic milk when Thelma walked in.

"*Hola*, Thelma Bean!" shouted Eugene. She rolled her eyes, but she secretly liked the nickname. "What's cooking, *chica*?"

"Not much, Eugene—is Alexander here yet?" she yelled over the whooshing and sputtering sounds of the hot milk.

"No, ma'am!"

"'Kay!"

Thelma scouted out an empty booth right by the window. It had a great view, especially on a blustery afternoon like this one. The walls inside Barney Beans were a warm butter yellow that made Thelma's stomach growl. Barney Beans was pretty busy with a rowdy group of senior citizens holding a book club meeting at the large back table. Thelma wondered what novel could possibly elicit such passionate opinions from Ms. Oaks, the typically soft-spoken librarian who was now pounding on the table to express herself. Well, thought Thelma, if anyone knows books, it's her.

She pulled out her notebook and flipped to a fresh page, penciling the words "Meeting Notes" in the header. Just as she completed the final s, the door jingled and Alexander jogged in. He was a little out of breath and looked sweaty. One of his sisters had probably made him run soccer drills with her again. Alexander's family was lousy with sisters—four of them, and all athletic. Poor Alexander was the runt of the pack, and the only boy. He hopped up onto the opposite side of the booth and plopped his backpack down beside him with a goofy, triumphant smile.

"Late!" Thelma said, pointing to her big blue watch.

Alexander furrowed his brow. "Yeah, right! It's 4:00 P.M. right now—I timed it perfectly!"

"No way! You—" Thelma's rebuttal was rudely interrupted by the clock tower chiming the first of four loud bongs, indicating that Alexander was, once again, correct. He sat back in his seat, smiling, and removed his glasses to clean them on the sleeve of his hoodie.

"Big deal," Thelma said. Secretly though, she felt totally double-crossed by her trusty wristwatch and took the opportunity to set it back two minutes.

Despite sometimes being a serious know-it-all, one of Alexander's main redeeming qualities was a keen appreciation for all of Thelma's schemes, the wilder, the better. When they were little kids, Thelma and Alexander had lived right next door to each other, which was ideal for rapid experimentation and invention. His family had moved across town two years ago, but their partnership was unbreakable. Alexander added vital brainpower to any operation, and he wasn't too shabby in the ideas department either.

Evidence: When Thelma wanted to build a Polynesian hanging-rope bridge between their two houses, not only was he there to advise on which knots would hold up strongest, but he also volunteered to beta test it—which resulted in an unfortunate twisted ankle. When she attempted to create a full-scale Viking longship in Clock Tower Pond, Alexander created some very sophisticated blueprints to guide the process—until Henry Bee ordered his daughter to "cease and desist."

In fact, both projects were thwarted by Thelma's dad, who shared her enterprising spirit but possessed a more grounded sensibility—and respect for local law.

"I had a thought about scaling Town Hall," said Alexander with a flash of inspiration in his big brown eyes. Thelma leaned in with anticipation. "We climb up to the top ... from the inside" he whispered the last words excitedly.

"Yes!" Thelma yelped, grabbing her pen, "The secret stairs? You think we can gain access?"

"Right up to the cupola ... I think." Alexander scrunched his nose and tilted his head, "Maybe. I've drafted a plan."

Eugene ambled over to the table. His walk always looked a little like dancing. "Hey, *que pasa* with your vanilla orchid project? Anything happen?" asked Eugene, propping a hand on his hip.

Thelma shook her head, "Not yet."

"All right, you keep me updated. I'm going to be *muy soprendido* if that thing blooms." He looked at Thelma with raised eyebrows.

"Surprised!" Thelma shouted triumphantly.

"Yeah, you got it!" he laughed and high-fived Thelma. "Miss is gonna be fluent *en espanol* before you know it," he said to Alexander.

"Nice!" said Alexander with a grin. Thelma didn't know how impressed her friend actually was. Alexander was a language whiz.

A few years ago, when he felt a desire to connect more with his heritage and culture, he started to learn Nipmuc, the language of his family's tribe. Alexander could go on for hours on his theory of language—how the world is shaped for us by the way we name it. Pretty deep stuff, but Thelma had listened intently.

Alexander had continued to study and practice Nipmuc as the youngest member of his group. He loved the experience so much that obscure languages became a kind of hobby for him. He said that it made him feel connected to history in a way that nothing else did.

So basically, Alexander had no problem mastering an incredibly subtle and complex tongue only known to a handful of people in the world, but Thelma expected him to be impressed by her learning a few phrases in Spanish.

Eugene presented two small mugs of spicy hot chocolate—Thelma's with a little whipped cream on top, "The usual, I presume?"

"Thanks, Eugene!" Thelma said as she took the hot mug in her hands. Eugene's spicy hot chocolate always tasted like heaven. She closed her eyes and took a big long whiff before letting herself sip.

Thelma imagined herself transported to a hut along the Amazon River ...

A sultry night. Outside—the ferocious river. The darkness teems with shrieking animal societies. Around an orange fire, a sandpapery shaman is dressed in faded brown cloth. He mixes a heady potion to bestow the drinker with extra years of life. The only person brave enough to try it is Thelma Bee, world traveler, scientist, and all-around excellent adventurer who has way better friends than dumb Jenny Sullivan and would never wear an "I hate math homework" T-shirt out of self respect. Thelma Bee sticks out her terracotta mug to receive the potion and then lifts it to her mouth. She takes the first, fateful sip. As the hot liquid runs down her throat ...

"Thelma?"

She opened her eyes to see Alexander waving a napkin in her face.

"You got whipped cream on your nose," he said.

"Oh, thanks." She wiped her face.

Eugene wore his old Barney Beans apron and a blue polo shirt with a patch that read "RVPS." That stood for Riverfish Valley Paranormal Society. One of Eugene's favorite pastimes was ghost hunting.

"Hey," Alexander hollered to Eugene, who was removing a half-eaten muffin from an empty table "Do you guys have an investigation tonight?"

RVPS held investigations every so often to scope out reportedly haunted locations and gather evidence about paranormal activity.

"Sure do! Tonight we're meeting at 10:00 P.M. Heading over to Magistrate's Manse in Cooktown. Have you heard of it?"

Eugene's eyes got wide and excited when he talked about ghost hunting. Thelma was pretty sure they'd never actually caught a ghost on camera or anything, but it was still something her friend was very passionate about.

"Um … I don't think so …" Alexander ruffled his brow.

"Oh—wait, just wait a sec …" Eugene ran past the table of shouting book club seniors, back to the storage room. Over the din of conflicting literary opinions, he shouted, "You're gonna like this one!"

When he emerged, he was wearing a metal contraption on his head. Alexander yelped with delight and shot out of his seat like a rocket. He lived for weird gadgets. The helmet was a large asymmetrical silver dome with black panels on the side and wires running down to a walkie-talkie-looking thing that Eugene held in his hand.

"Nice!" Alexander stood on his toes to try to get a good look.

"What is that?" Thelma asked. "What does it do?"

"What?" Eugene yelled from under his helmet. Apparently it prevented him from hearing anything.

"Eugene! Take off the—" they motioned for him to remove the contraption from his head, which he did.

"Oh, yeah, right! Sorry about that. I just got this in the mail today. I wasn't expecting it in time for tonight's investigation, so you can imagine I'm pretty excited to take her out for a test drive!"

"What does it do?" Thelma asked.

"Well, as you know, most spirits—not all of them, but most of them—are very quiet talkers," he said. Thelma actually didn't know that and wondered silently if it was indeed a fact that could be quantified. Regardless, she grabbed her notebook to scribble down the new info. Header:

Ghost Facts (according to E)

—she underlined that qualifier. Of course she believed that Eugene believed what he was saying, but she'd never engaged in a ghost investigation or, for that matter, seen any hard proof.

Eugene went on, "Part of

our investigation is to record the ghosts with very sensitive microphones. When we go over the evidence, we play it back with the volume way up to see if we can decipher what the ghost is saying."

Thelma and Alexander nodded.

"Yeah. So this little baby here—this is going to save me a step. Instead of recording the ghosties and then listening to them the next day, this helmet has super-sensitive microphones built right into it, and this new technology magnifies the sound automatically here—" he pointed at the dome "—so the voices can reach me immediately." He pointed to his ears.

"Brilliant!"

"Totally," said Alexander, "As long as the ghosts don't think you are, you know, a robot or alien or something."

"You've got to tell us how it goes tonight! I'll bet you'll … you know, catch a huge ghost?" said Thelma with a question in her voice.

Eugene laughed, "Thelma Bean, we never really want to catch a spirit!"

"Oh, OK, so what do you do with them?" she asked.

"We're hunting for evidence, for communication with the other side, *chica*. Like …" Eugene's eyes got dreamy, "… like answers to the big questions, you know? What happens on the other side?" He laughed a little, "What in the world would I do with a ghost if I caught one? It's not a fish!"

It was a fair question that Thelma hadn't considered. She'd watched a movie as a kid where ghost hunters kept their catches in a big ghost tank, which was, upon consideration, totally impractical. "Huh," she said. "Well, I hope you catch some huge ghost communication tonight then."

The little bell on the counter dinged twice, and Eugene turned to help his customer.

"That's a deal, ma'am," he shouted over his shoulder.

"Truly amazing." Alexander shook his head from side to side in wonder. He pushed his glasses back up the bridge of his nose.

"Yeah," said Thelma.

What happens on the other side? Eugene's words swirled like cotton candy in her mind. She gripped her pen and pressed it to her notebook.

QUESTION: What happens on the other side?

Mega-Deer and Dokeys

Back home, after a dinner of homemade pizza with baked sweet potato and onions, Thelma and her dad split dishwashing duties and then headed to the computer to see if anything new had come in from the Appalachian Trail. Mom was pretty far off the grid during this expedition. Her emails were few and far between, and they'd only been able to reach her on the phone once in the two weeks she'd been gone. But tonight, to their excitement, there was a new email from Mom:

```
From: Mary.Goosefoot.Bee@mailmail.com

To: Henry.Bee@mailmail.com, thelma.la.gran
@mailmail.com

Re: Hello from the trail!
```

Dearest Henry and Thelma,

I'm happy to report that we are currently warm and safe and staying in a tiny town in western Tennessee called Tankerel, with a wonderful family by the name of Dokey. Point of interest: Mr. and Mrs. Dokey have named their children the following: France, Germany, Italy, and baby Spain. I've thought it queer since learning this information but am afraid to ask for further explanation. I don't want to insult my hosts, but I am very curious! My first impressions, however, are that none of these children belong to their titular nationality. Will report more as I gather better intelligence.

In Mega-deer news:

The weather is fine, and the trail has not yet tested my spirit—or my knees—for which I'm exceedingly grateful. Yesterday, intern Brenda found a promising trail for us to follow, and from the prints, I think there's something really interesting going on. I won't be sure until we can collect some DNA, but there is cause to suspect Mega-deer is a long-lost descendent of the Irish Elk! It sounds crazy, but as you both know—anything is possible!

I shall see you both in two short weeks, and
that makes the rocky trail seem not so very
long at all.

Lots of love and many, many kisses,

Mom

"Irish elk," Thelma mused out loud.

"It'll be great to have Mom home soon." Dad's eyes
were soft and filled with missing her. "When she gets
back, we'll go ahead and take that trip to Lake Winnemusket, I think."

"Really?" Thelma squealed triumphantly and
hugged her dad.

"Yeah! I already reserved a cabin for the three of us
right on the water."

"Oh, Dad, this is amazing, truly amazing! I have it
all worked out. I think I can even borrow Alexander's
telescope. It's not waterproof, but I have some ideas …
Do you think we can rent a canoe?"

"Done."

Ghost Facts

(OBSERVED)

Thelma floated through her evening routine that night, visions of underwater anthropology dancing through her head. It started raining outside as she changed into her pajamas. The drops made a loud, rhythmic sound on her bedroom window—rut dut dut dut dut—and she imagined herself back in time, in a low pulsing circle of Wampanoag warriors.

The strong-limbed men do the warrior's grass dance as her shoulders thump with the unrelenting beat. Her feet stomp. Waves of percussion roll through her whole body, making Thelma Bee, world traveler and excellent adventurer, one with the dance and the warrior spirit. She reaches up to the big black sky to summon the thunder, thump, thump, thump . . .

Thelma's solo dance was interrupted by a

light clinking sound. When she opened her eyes she saw someone dart into her upstairs bathroom.

Thelma froze.

"Dad?"

No answer.

She called for her father again, louder this time, and heard him yell up from the kitchen.

"Yeah! Thel? Do you need something?"

"Um … no. You're not in the upstairs bathroom, are you?" she asked, knowing very well that he was not.

"I'm in the kitchen just cleaning up a little. Are you heading to bed? It's about that time …" His voice trailed off.

"OK." Thelma was quiet, her eyes locked on the dark strip of space between the bathroom's blue door and the wall. It was just an empty space, but cool fingers of fear and curiosity gripped her imagination. She thought she could sense something hiding inside the space. It was full of dark electricity. She knew what was usually in the bathroom—a toilet, a shower, a sink—but as Thelma's gaze focused on the deepening blackness of the threshold, it seemed to pulse and crackle with danger.

Someone was in there, or at least that's what she thought she saw. But how was that possible? The door was barely open, and it usually made a terrible creaking sound when it swung. Thelma hadn't heard any loud creaking.

Slowly she padded across the floor, trying to make

as little noise as possible. The rain poured outside. She wrapped her fingers around the doorknob, her heart feeling like a bouncy ball in her chest. With a deep, determined breath, she swung the door open and flicked on the light switch.

Nothing. Thelma scanned the room: sink, radiator, toilet with fuzzy pink cover, shower curtain ...

Shower curtain. It was closed.

That meant that he or she or it had to be hiding in the shower. Thelma steadied herself and reached down to grab the wooden hilt of the plunger—she held it out in front of her as a makeshift sword.

1 ... 2 ... 3 ... pull!

Thelma stood in front of an utterly empty shower, hunched like a gargoyle with a plunger ready to strike. There was nothing there. Well, there was some shampoo and a loofah, but no predators, runaway brides, or wolfmen.

Still feeling a little shaky, Thelma decided to proceed with her nightly routine. She worried about just how vivid her imagination seemed to be, as she ran the faucet, waiting for warm water. She was thoroughly freaking herself out, and not in a fun way. Probably all that ghost talk with Eugene earlier, she thought. She squeezed a quarter-sized glob of Mrs. Easterly Down's Skin Healthifying Soap into her palm and worked it into a great white lather all over her face. She ignored the watched feeling. And the buzzing sound.

According to Thelma's mom, this soap stuff was

the secret to healthy, "elastic" skin. Thelma didn't understand why a person would want their skin to be elastic, but she did know that her mother was far and away the prettiest lady she'd ever met. Mom brought a whole stock of the soap back from New Zealand last summer, and Thelma had made a nightly ceremony out of lathering up her face. She didn't have her mom's flawless complexion or her amazing shiny red hair, but she did inherit Mary Bee's eyes, big and foggy-ocean blue.

Thelma tested the water with her fingers, and when it was warm enough, she scooped the fresh stream with both hands and splashed it all over until she was clean and wiped the excess water off with a fluffy hand towel.

She put her head to the side to shake out the excess water in her ears. The buzzing she'd been hearing ever since she walked into the bathroom seemed to be getting worse. She'd dismissed it as the light bulb, but all at once it grew and sharpened.

"Return."

A scared shock jolted Thelma's body. It was a voice. A voice that sounded only inches away. The word was spoken like a pointy jab.

That was not her dad. It did not come from downstairs.

Every particle in Thelma's body tensed. She darted sideways, eyes wide with shock. There was a long stretch of silence as she tried to control her breathing.

"Return." The sound felt like a violation against

her ears and she covered them with her hands out of instinct.

Thelma's heart pounded even faster, heavy like battle drum. The voice was a woman's voice, but there was nothing and nobody to her right or left. Then, creeping like steam from a hot shower, something took shape in the mirror.

The face was human—sort of. It was skeleton-thin with weedy hair and deep black pits where eyes should be. The lips curled; this time, the word was a demand.

"RETURN"

Thelma broke from the spell with a jump and a shriek and ran out of the bathroom, across the hall-way, and down the stairs faster than she realized her legs could go.

"DAD!!"

She rushed into the kitchen, where he was putting dishes back in the cupboard.

"Whoa! What's going on?"

Thelma shook. She stared at her father for a moment, a dishtowel flung casually over his shoul-der. "What" was a great question. What had just happened? What was that in the mirror? What did "return" mean?

"There's … uh …" She squashed her eyebrows together trying to think of the right way to communi-cate the situation. "… Dad, I saw something upstairs."

"Are you OK? What is it? Some kind of animal?" He grabbed his daughter's shoulders.

return

"A ... lady ... I think ..."
Thelma's brain was working fast
trying to come up with the right words.
"There's a stranger in the house? Thelma,
talk to me!"

"No! Yes. She's ... kind of just a face." She winced at
how silly her own words sounded. "Dad, I think I saw
a ghost. Upstairs." That was it, much more concise.
She exhaled.

They stood in silence for a moment as her father
put his hand to his head and massaged his temples.

"Bedtime," he said.

"Wha ...?"

"I said it's bedtime, Thelma Bee. You're very crafty.
What should we do? I suppose stay up late for a ghost
hunt? That'd suit you, wouldn't it?" he chuckled a little. "But it's time for you to get some rest."

"But, Dad! It's the truth! It was terrifying! She was
in the mirror in the bathroom right after I washed my
face—"

"C'mon, Thel, let's head up." He placed his hand on
her shoulder and led her up the stairs. She couldn't
believe this. Crafty? He thought she was being crafty?
First of all, how insulting. Second ... well, she was
very insulted.

Thelma protested all the way into her bed, but Henry just tucked her into her sheets tight, like a mummy.

"You got me before, honey, but I'm not falling for it this time. Although, as always—points for originality," he said and kissed her on the forehead. "Hey, tomorrow morning I'm going to reupholster that loveseat from today. Want to pick the fabric?"

Fabric? She couldn't believe this.

"Dad, I'm honestly not trying to pull a fast one here. Just look in the bathroom, OK?"

Dad sighed and nodded. He crossed the hall to the bathroom, which was still illuminated. He opened the door and stepped inside—Thelma could see him from her bed. He looked around.

"All clear in here, Thel," said Dad.

"Check the mirror," she yelled.

A moment of quiet as Dad scoped out the mirror, touching it, turning his head to get a better look. He walked back into Thelma's room, where she huddled beneath her sheets.

"I can't see anything at all," he said, "I'm not saying you didn't see anything, I'm saying I can't see anything. OK?"

"Fine." She was in disbelief that her father, a reasonable man typically, could be this insensitive. It was true, she'd devised some really elaborate plans to stay up all night in the past, but that was in elementary school, and this was for real.

"I love you," he kissed her head, "Goodnight, Thel."

He got up and closed the bathroom door on his way down the hall.

As soon as he was out of sight, Thelma reached up and grabbed for the mini flashlight that she kept tied to a long shoelace on her bedpost. She clicked it on and propped it on her nightstand. In her notebook, under "Ghost Facts (according to E)" she created a new heading:

GHOST FACTS: OBSERVED

· Observed spirit's voice was not quiet.

- Seemed to be female.

- Can appear in mirrors.

- Said "Return"—what does this mean?

- Was generally really unpleasant and even probably terrible.

Thelma tried to think of more but she was still a little shaky.

"OK," she thought, trying to calm herself, "just fall asleep—we'll deal with this in the morning." After all, she was acquainted with one of the only bona fide amateur ghost hunters in Riverfish. Eugene would be able to shed some light on all this. Also, Alexander would have input on the scientific implications here.

The prospect of a full-blown paranormal investigation in her house should have been an exciting one. Thelma usually got a good adrenaline feeling when a new experiment hatched inside her brain. She knew she should be excited, but she felt heavy instead. She tried to psych herself up, to loosen the big knot in her stomach. Maybe they could get the whole group from RVPS to come and stake out her bathroom—cameras, crazy microphone hats, the whole nine yards.

Eventually, she drifted off to sleep with a brain full of ideas for the next day's adventure. Dad would see that she wasn't faking it. This was business, real and scientific. He'd be lucky if she even had time to work on reupholstering the loveseat. But probably, she thought, she'd pick a lime green fabric. That would look cool.

As exhaustion crept over Thelma's body, she ruled out possible scientific causes for her experience: a drop in barometric pressure, soap in her eyes, hallucinogenic onions ...

She drifted off counting improbable hypotheses instead of sheep.

Gravity and Anti-Gravity

(EXPERIENCED)

At 3:00 A.M., a strong, cold wind blew through Thelma's bedroom window. She woke with a start, confused. She had definitely shut it tightly earlier during the heavy rain, so it was pretty peculiar that the window was open now. Thelma's skin prickled. Her hair almost blew out of her loose ponytail as she sat up and looked around the room.

Thelma scurried over, and placed two hands on the window to force it closed, but it was stuck. The whipping wind made it hard to steady herself against the frame. Was Riverfish expecting a hurricane? A surprise severe weather event seemed kind of unreasonable in the age of Doppler radar, satellites, and ten-day outlooks.

But then, focusing her gaze out the window,

Thelma observed the trees outside. Her stomach dropped—the trees weren't swaying. They were perfectly still.

There was a brief moment of quiet. Confused and beginning to panic, she wiped the escaped hair wisps away from her face. At that moment, a forceful gust of black air knocked her over like a punch to the gut.

A scream caught in Thelma's throat as she looked up and saw the figure of a woman hovering just inches from the ceiling. The neck was bent at an unnatural angle, and the hair that covered the figure's face shimmered with electricity. The body was crooked, and adorned in a long white dress. Thelma was motionless. She stared breathlessly but was determined not to show fear.

"What do you want?" she yelled over the whistling wind.

The figure lifted its right arm, face still hidden. Thelma didn't want to see that face again. The wardrobe doors whipped open, spitting clothes and shoes all over the room. This creature was very angry. The woman in the dress slowly lifted its chin, and Thelma winced, but didn't hide. There it was. The same horrifying image Thelma remembered from the bathroom mirror. Somewhere in the black holes of those eyes lived a million terrifying questions. Electric sparks crackled dimly in the dark.

Lightheaded, Thelma felt the gravity in the room change. She felt as if she was spinning and she willed herself not to pass out. The figure pointed directly at her as though there was vision in the black pits of its eyes. Thelma huddled under her bedroom window and hugged her knees. The figure reached out its hands towards her neck and Thelma felt an invisible frost spread across her skin—her mom's opal necklace was ice cold. She held the stone close to her and put her head to her chest, wishing harder than she'd ever wished that her mom were there.

"Reeeeeturn!"

The wind intensified. It whirred around the woman until it formed a twister that enveloped her completely. The figure disappeared inside the cyclone.

Stillness swallowed the room in a deafening quiet. Thelma's gaze darted from corner to corner. Her forehead was damp with sweat as she anticipated what would come next. A crash came from downstairs.

Dad. Her breath stopped. She had to get to her father. Thelma picked herself up off of the floor and crept to the top of the stairs with nervous feet.

"Dad? Dad!" she yelled down, but there was no answer. She set one foot in front of the other down the stairwell, so familiar in daylight, but now a forbidding passage. She heard more movement—it came from the dining room. She grasped the railing like a lifeline and made her way to the bottom step.

In the blue-black light of the very early morning, Thelma's dad stood by the dining room table with his glasses off, and eyes half-closed.

"Dad! Daddy, wake up!" Thelma felt panic. Her father wasn't a sleepwalker, and it chilled her to see him there, motionless and towering, without any sparkle or personality in his eyes. She was afraid to go near him, but then a wave of deeper fear swallowed her whole. The fear that if she didn't wake him up right now, something really bad was going to happen.

Thelma put her chin to her chest and rushed into her father like a battering ram, making a noise that was half war cry and half whimper. The whole force of her small form smashed into her father, but he was like a brick wall. He didn't budge or wince, nor did his face register any feeling at all. Thelma hit the floor with a painful thud, and it wasn't until she was there, looking up at her dad with tears welling in her eyes, that she noticed it sitting right in the middle of their dining room table. That mysterious lady's jewelry box.

Rage rose up inside of Thelma. This thing was trouble. And how on earth did it get there? She knew for a fact that it was not in the house while they were eating homemade pizza, reading Mom's email, or making canoe plans. The shop was located at least a quarter mile down the street in the town center. Had her father brought it home to inspect for some reason? No way. At any rate, he never conducted random antique inspections in the middle of the night. She turned to her dad.

"Dad ... please wake up." Thelma clutched the sleeves of her pajamas in her sweating hands and brought them up to her face, half wanting to hide from her father in this strange state.

Henry's chin jerked up to the ceiling. After watching him stand lifeless and limp, his violent motion was so unexpected that Thelma nearly jumped out of her skin. With equal speed and strength, he turned his head to the left so that his gaze fell on her family's photo collection on their mantel.

Thelma's favorite picture of her parents stood there. It had been taken just after Henry and Mary were married. In it, they both looked beautiful. Mom was gorgeous in a simple white dress. Dad, dapper in a gray suit, stared at her with awe and devotion in his bespectacled eyes. Thelma loved looking at the picture, especially when she missed Mom.

In the weird light of not-quite-morning, her dad stared at the photo. His gaze intensified. Then, the sound of glass breaking. The wedding photo didn't just crack, it shattered. Shards flew like tiny bullets through the air, and Thelma screamed. The rest of the mantel's pictures followed suit, exploding one by one, with glass flying everywhere.

All she could do was cower on the floor, covering her face. Her dad turned around and Thelma uncovered her face to meet his gaze. The eyes were wide open now, glaring at her. They were entirely white. His mouth opened, and the voice that emerged was dreadfully familiar to Thelma, but it wasn't her dad's. It was a voice that emerged from a sea of harsh buzzing.

"RETURN"

"Let him go!!" Thelma screamed with tears running zigzag patterns down her cheeks. "What do you want from me?"

In an instant, Henry collapsed onto the floor, the full weight of his body making a loud thump.

Thelma's breath came in shallow snatches. She was afraid to approach her dad's body. She didn't want his face to be someone else's.

Henry started to shift slowly on the floor, his hand rising up to touch his head, which had taken a serious bump in the ordeal.

"Thelma?" He squinted and tried to focus.

"Dad? Is that you?" she whispered.

"Thelma, what's going on? Why are you down here? Why am I …"

"Dad!" She rushed to his side as he sat up. "Dad, something's here. It took a hold of you. We have to go!"

"What do you mean, 'took a hold of me'? I'm … I was sleepwalking, I think."

Thelma tried to help her father off of the floor, when she noticed goose bumps rising up on her arm. It was getting cold very fast.

A heavy, slow scraping sound pulled their attention to the front door. Dad grabbed onto Thelma as they watched their large bookcase drag heavily, by itself, across the living room floor and come to a stop in front of the door. Similar movements could be heard throughout the house. In the kitchen, upstairs, even below them in the cellar, she heard the scraping noise of furniture moving itself.

"Whoa," Dad gasped.

"She's not going to let us out."

"What the—" Henry was now fully awake.

Thelma noticed that something strange was happening with the jewelry box. A small stream of smoke, thin and gray, escaped from the keyhole beneath the two interlocked brass hands. The smoke traveled in a direct line to her dad and wrapped itself like a vine around his wrist.

"Come on!" Thelma pulled her father away from the chest, but he didn't budge.

Henry grimaced, panic in his dark brown eyes. "I can't move, Thel." Thelma saw her father's trapped wrist and hand start to disintegrate, becoming smoke.

"No!" She screamed, and rushed to the box. She had to destroy it. She grabbed it with both hands but yelped in pain—the thing was extremely hot. Her father's arm, inch by inch, turned from flesh and bone to smoke, and the smoke was sucked right back into the box. Though she was freaking out completely, there was no time for shock and disbelief. Thelma looked for anything she could find, a bat, an axe, anything. She rushed to the kitchen and got a mallet. She'd smash the thing. When she got back to the dining room, her father was halfway gone already.

"Thelma ..." her father said, eyes wide with panic. "I'm sorry. I love you! ..."

Thelma raised the mallet over her head and with all the strength in her body brought it down on the box. It felt just like concrete, and a quick examination of the mallet's head revealed that it had been splintered by the impact.

"Thelma, your mother ..." were the last words out

of her dad's mouth before he was taken wholly into the small, antique box that he had bought for one hundred dollars cash just hours ago.

Thelma looked wildly around the room, and then back to the box. What had just happened? Where was her dad? The room spun and she felt as though she would throw up or faint. She gripped the edge of the table so hard her fingers started to turn purple. Her face was wet with tears before she realized that she was sobbing. Grasping at the only solution she could think of, she counted backwards.

10 Mississippi

The room spun. Sweat ran down her neck. Nausea crept from her belly up to her throat.

9 Mississippi

"Breathe in," she commanded herself, "Breathe." Air filled up her lungs.

8 Mississippi

The box, the awful, cursed box. She'd try to destroy it again. Throw it into a fire maybe … but what if her dad was really in there?

7 Mississippi

The police. That's who people called in emer-gencies, right? But they would think she was crazy. Even she thought she might be crazy at this moment in time.

6 Mississippi

Mom. She would definitely know what to do. But the only way to get in touch was email, and she might not see that for days. Why was Mom gone now when Thelma needed her? She was always gone

5 Mississippi

Thelma reached out to the box with tentative, shaking hands and she found it cool. She hugged it tightly and bent her head into her arms as a fresh wave of helplessness took her down.

"Daddy," she whimpered.

A long time ago, Thelma had watched a documentary about outer space on TV. She remembered a physicist explaining gravity and anti-gravity. There was a force on earth keeping everything together and another force pushing everything apart. And someday maybe anti-gravity would win the wrestling match and then everything and everybody would burst into tiny particles. Nothing would be anymore. She wanted so badly at that moment to simply come apart, to explode into nothing.

By the time she got to 4 *Mississippi*, awash in exhausted tears, her body and brain finally gave up, and Thelma passed out.

Collection of Evidence

(DODGING THE COOKIE LADY)

When she woke, it was day. The sun streamed into the room and illuminated the chaos in Thelma's house. A giant bookcase still blocked the front door. Glass shards still decorated the dining room, like a glitter bomb went off. In the middle of the table, just inches away from her hands, sat the wooden box with two small brass knobs in the shape of interlocking hands, and one keyhole. Dad was still gone.

Reality came crashing back to her. What she saw, what she actually lived through, hadn't been imagined. This was a real mess, her house was actually torn apart and her father was gone. Thelma stood up and felt her head, rubbed her arms, just to make sure she was still there. For a moment she didn't know what to do. But through the confusion, one name came through clearly: Alexander.

She didn't think she could explain things over the phone, and she didn't want to try. She just asked him to come to her house as fast as he could.

"Take your bike," she said, "and if you can't take your bike, maybe run."

Alexander was there in less than five minutes. Thelma heard a knock at the front door and smacked her forehead with the palm of her hand, realizing that it was still very effectively blocked by a piece of furniture at least twice her height.

"Alexander!"

"Yeah, I'm here, Thelma. Let me in! What's going on?"

"Just … ugh, use the window."

"Huh? Like, climb in the window?"

"Yeah! Go over to the right side of the house, OK?"

"OK!"

In the kitchen there were two very large windows above the countertop. Thelma opened both of them and, figuring that things couldn't get much more torn apart, punched out the screens.

"Here you go!"

Alexander climbed through the window onto the counter with a little trouble.

"Was there some unscheduled construction?" he joked. Thelma's expression was so troubled, though, he quickly sobered.

"Thelma, did your family get robbed? You've got to call the police! Have you touched anything? You shouldn't touch anything—that way they can dust for fingerprints and run them through the ..." he searched for words as he looked around in shock, "the ... database to generate a suspect list. I can't believe this happened! There hasn't been a burglary in River-fish since—"

"We didn't get robbed," Thelma interrupted.

"What?" he looked around, "Thelma, where's your dad?" Alexander was truly befuddled.

At that, Thelma's eyes welled up again, but this time she mustered the strength to hold back the tears.

"Alexander, I think my dad's gone."

"Gone?" his voice softened in concern, "Gone where?"

"It's a crazy story, and you have to promise that you will believe me," she said sternly.

"I promise."

"Because I won't tell you anything about it if you aren't going to believe me. You can just leave right now ..." Her anxiety was starting to choke out her voice.

"Thelma! Geez, come on!" Alexander grabbed her, shaking shoulders. "I am going to believe you. I always believe you." That was true, she knew it. He took her hand in his and squeezed it. Usually that kind of thing would make Thelma uncomfortable enough to pull it back, but today she really needed the reassurance.

They sat down on two stools next to the counter and Thelma told Alexander the whole story—from miserable old lady to shattered picture frames. One thing she knew from her study of science was that things that seem impossible are usually not. Space travel, multiple dimensions, even mountain ranges on Pluto—all pretty wild ideas. But what had happened last night was truly beyond belief.

"First things first," Alexander said, "Email your mom. She might not get it for a few days but you've got to try. After that we clean up, OK?"

She was dazed. He persisted, "Thelma are you with me? Are you OK?"

"Yeah. I'll get the computer," she said.

Thelma didn't exactly feel relieved, but she did feel less out of control. After all the panic and fear and the not knowing what to do, Alexander was there to help with a plan. Yes, she thought, first things first.

From: thelma.la.gran@mailmail.com

To: Mary.Goosefoot.Bee@mailmail.com

Re: Emergency!

Mom, something bad happened. It's hard to explain, but you have to come home now. Please. Come home as fast as you can.

I love you,

Thelma

Alexander went from room to room, opening windows and removing various pieces of furniture from doorways and windows. He also took on the job of re-hanging all of Thelma's clothes and re-pairing up all the shoes littered around the bedroom.

Thelma got out the broom and dustpan and began the job of sweeping up the bits of glass from the dining room floor. The scene played on repeat in her mind, the way her father's eyes turned white and that awful voice escaping his lips. What did that ghost have against her family? Why would it want to kidnap her father into that old jewelry box?

She picked up the wedding picture. Her mom and dad were so happy and in love there. She brushed the broken glass off the photo and into the trash, but the tiny shards of glass were impossible to avoid. As she pulled one out of her hand she bled a little. Then she noticed all the minuscule sparkling bits in her palms. She stared at her hands, not knowing what to do, then walked to the sink and ran them under cold water.

What was Dad trying to tell her in those last moments? Something about her mother—but what? She dried her hands with the dishtowel carefully, not knowing if she was pushing the glass bits deeper into her hands or brushing them off.

Thelma thought of how devastated Mom would be if she knew Dad was gone. Then she thought about how differently things could have played out if her mom was home for once instead of in the field. Her mom's work was very important, and Thelma understood that. She knew she was being unfair. But there was a part of her that felt angry. It didn't feel like a small part.

Mom would probably be furious when she got home, Thelma imagined. Thelma had allowed her father to be kidnapped out of their own house, right in front of her face. Thelma was a giant rubber-band ball of emotions and none of them were good—mad at Mom, disappointed in herself, gutted that her dad wasn't there to make things OK. But there had to be a way to get him back. And she'd find it.

Thelma looked over at the antique box. She was going to open this thing up whether it wanted to open or not. She looked at her hands and made a few tentative fists. She didn't feel any glass bits, so she resolved to pretend like they were all out. She grabbed the box with both hands and started pulling at the handle. She grunted and pounded with all of her strength and a lot of rage. Finally, she threw the whole thing against the wall with a frustrated scream. Alexander heard her from upstairs and came to see what was wrong. He discovered Thelma, red-faced and breathing hard, with her hands on her hips, the box lying sideways on the floor across the room, and a dent in the living room wall.

"There has to be a way to open this thing!" she yelled to the ceiling. "He's in there! We have to get him out!" She turned around and kicked the wall behind her with so much force she really hurt her toes. "Ow!

Monkey dung!" she threw her head back and grunted, plopping down on the floor.

"The records." Alexander's face lit up, registering an idea. "Thelma, you said that the lady came in yesterday to sell your dad the box, right?"

"Yeah," she said as she wiggled her toes painfully. At least they still worked.

"Well, he had to have written down the transaction, don't you think? Maybe he wrote her a check or something and he's got the receipt on file?"

"Cash," Thelma huffed. "She made a whole big deal about cash. And come to think of it, I did ask her where she was from and she got very weird about it."

"Weird how? What did she say?"

"Elsewhere," Thelma said, impersonating the lady's nasty tone.

"That … yeah. That doesn't help."

"Well," she said, "let's check the office anyway. Maybe there's at least a name."

Thelma walked back up to her room to get dressed and grab her notebook. Alexander had cleaned up really efficiently. He'd also made her bed, which was something she herself barely ever did. It looked good, she noted. Maybe worth a try once in a while. Probably not, though.

Thelma changed out of her pajamas and into jeans and sneakers. Checking herself in the mirror, she grimaced a little. Her hair was a knotted brown disaster. She struggled it back into a ponytail before heading downstairs and out the kitchen window with her best friend and co-investigator.

Bee's Very Unusual Antiques was a five-minute walk from Thelma's house on Maple Avenue. It happened to be a beautiful sunny autumn day in Riverfish. It was the kind of day that Thelma usually loved the most.

On their walk, she and Alexander saw Jonas Newlittle, proprietor of Newlittle Realty, and Riverfish selectman. He was flyering the town with Applekin Festival ads.

Jonas waved a delighted hello to Alexander and Thelma as they scurried by. She wished she could enjoy the day, but instead she was wracked with the heaviest feeling she'd ever felt. She couldn't get the lead weight out of her belly. She bet if she stepped on a scale it would say "1,000 pounds. Please step off, you're going to break me."

Their best hope, it seemed, would be filed away in one of Henry Bee's cupboards. Thelma reached into her pocket for the fifth time, just to make sure that she had her keys.

As they approached Bee's Antiques, Mrs. Edelstein appeared around the corner and made Thelma jump. She hugged the antique box tight to her chest while trying to give the appearance that nothing strange was going on.

"Thelma!" Mrs. Edelstein hollered, smiling.

She was waiting outside of the shop in brightly colored running shorts with a sweatband tight around her forehead. She wasn't jogging so much as hopping in place. Mrs. Edelstein also had a large basket of cookies wrapped up in packs of four and tied delicately with red curly ribbon.

"Oh, and hi there, Alexander—how are you today?" she asked, distracted momentarily.

"Good!" Poor Alexander was not much of an actor. In an attempt to hide the urgency of their errand, and the inconvenience of having to stop, his words came out in an overenthusiastic yelp. Mrs. Edelstein looked at him sideways for a moment.

"I just got through running with your sister," she said.

"Oh? Uh … which one?" he asked with a crack in his voice.

"Lana, of course!" she smiled, "The Riverfish Running Club had a great few laps around the water today! Your sister really zooms, doesn't she? These old legs can't keep up!"

Lana really did zoom, as a matter of fact. Not only was she top ten in the state, but she had also just set a record time in the Hassanamisco Nipmuc Youth Council's annual 5K. She was kind of a town treasure.

"Yeah," Alexander said, forcing a smile. "She sure zooms."

"Anyhow." The hopping baker turned her attention back to Thelma. "I've been waiting for your father, dear. Is he around?"

This was a moment Thelma hadn't prepared for. How was she going to explain her father's mysterious absence? She couldn't just tell the truth—no one would believe her. Her cheeks got hot.

"He went to meet my mom in Tennessee," she blurted.

Mrs. Edelstein furrowed her brow and turned her head sideways, her curls bouncing over her sweatband.

"He left you all alone here, Thelma? That doesn't sound at all like Henry…"

Thelma's words rushed from her nervous mouth like an unstoppable waterfall. "No—well, yes, for a little bit. He left this morning. Really, it was an emergency. I'm going to catch a train this afternoon and meet both of them. We're staying with the Dokeys. The um … Dokeys of Appalachia. It's a long story. Anyway—" Thelma switched the antique to one arm and grabbed the basket of cookies with her other. She beamed a cheerful, forced smile. "I'll take these and set them up inside. Thank you so much, Mrs. Edelstein!!"

Still with the same crinkled, thoughtful expression on her face, Mrs. Edelstein nodded and continued her mid-jog hopping rhythm. "OK, then, Miss Bee. You— you just let me know if you need anything. I'll see you all when you get back from the, er, Dokeys then."

"Thanks! We really appreciate it! Have a great jog, bye!" Thelma waited until Mrs. Edelstein was a few feet away before digging the keys out of her pocket and unlocking the door. She pushed it open with her shoulder and they rushed in. Once inside they shut the door and locked it. Thelma made sure that

the side of the sign that faced the street read "CLOSED."

"Who are the Dokeys?" Alexander asked once they were safely inside.

"Don't worry about it." Thelma climbed two steps onto a step stool, reached up, and pulled a thin, silver chain. When she let go, a warm light flooded Bee's Very Unusual Antiques.

Thelma had grown up in the shop. When she was very little, her mom and dad created a magical (though sometimes quite dusty) world behind the large red door at 22 Main Street. That was ten years ago, when Thelma was only one, so her earliest memories had lots to do with the tall wood-beamed ceilings and a feeling that there were endless discoveries around every corner. When she was just learning to walk, Thelma bobbled around in an improvised playpen made of antique couches and ottomans from various time periods. She once got in trouble for using an 1882 edition of *Walden* by Thoreau as a teething surface. The drool decreased the book's value substantially.

In the beginning, the shop was mainly full of the treasures that Dad and Mom collected around the globe. The space filled up with wonderful curiosities, like a towering cuckoo clock from Dusseldorf, a brilliant red-and-gold tapestry from New Mexico that covered an entire wall, and dainty teacups from Tokyo painted with tiny pink magnolias. The shop had always been—and still was—a very special place.

Thelma loved each piece in the shop. If she couldn't learn the story behind an item, she'd make one up. She'd decided that one particular pair of ratty old shoes were priceless because they belonged to a medieval duchess, and a plain wooden picture frame was wrought from the same wood used to construct the first covered wagons on the Oregon Trail. Over time the collection grew and shrank with trades, sales, and purchases, but no matter what was in it, Thelma always felt that the shop was a second home.

Standing in that beloved place, she suddenly snapped back to reality and felt, once again, the heavy pit in her belly. Her dad was missing—that's why they were here. Alexander headed to the office, and she scuttled to catch up with him.

"Not the most organized filing system," Alexander murmured as he sifted through a large blue folder that was labeled "Things Bought for Shop: Autumn."

Thelma leaned over Alexander's shoulder trying to catch a glimpse of something worthwhile. There were receipts, copies of checks, but nothing that jumped out as a clue.

"I'm looking for something that has yesterday's date on it. There's just so much stuff in here; you'd think it would be right on top."

"My dad has an alphabetical system," Thelma said.

"By name?"

"No, by object."

"That doesn't make sense."

"Sure it does. If it's a mixing bowl, it'll be under *m* for mixing bowl, galoshes under *g*, xylophone under ..."

"X." Alexander looked up at Thelma and smiled.

"I know that," she said clenching her jaw.

"This system is pretty flawed," Alexander pushed his glasses up onto the bridge of his nose and kept searching.

"Well, I'm sorry it's not up to your standards, Alexander. I'm really sorry if you think I'm dumb and my dad's system is dumb," she snapped. She knew she was being overly sensitive, and Alexander meant no offense, but she didn't care. She clutched her necklace and rubbed it with her thumb.

Alexander looked up at her with raised eyebrows.

"Sorry, Thelma, geez. It's fine ... there's a kind of chaotic beauty in his system." He nudged her arm. "Also, if it's one thing I do not think you are, it's ... shy." He rushed to add, "But! But, if there's a second thing that I definitely, definitely don't think you are, it's dumb. You're one of the smartest people I know."

That was a big compliment coming from Alexander, and Thelma suddenly felt herself blush in an alto-gether different way. She made a mental note to add "face un-reddener" to her list of potential inventions. She took a deep breath and pointed to the folder.

"Well, look for the jewelry box," she said.

"OK, *j* for jewelry box …"

"Hmm … no. Try *s*. It's a very small box," she offered.

Alexander sighed and shook his head. Thelma detected a little eye roll. He found the *s* section. There were papers for "Silver earrings: Egypt 1910," "Salad spinner: Pennsylvania 1993," and, just as Thelma had thought, "Small wooden jewelry box: Massachusetts 18th century." That last one had the right date on it as well as a few notes. Jackpot.

Sweeping her arm across her father's desk to clear space, Thelma laid out the piece of paper her dad had folded in two just yesterday. The first line read, "Paid in cash—$100," and under that he had scribbled a few notes from his conversation with the strange lady.

"Family heirloom—Massachusetts—sometime in the late 18th century (need to verify). Cherry, maple finish, small brass knobs in the shape of interlocking hands. Keyhole beneath knobs. Burned-in markings on the bottom, inscription—unknown language (need to verify)."

At the bottom was Henry Bee's trademark signature, a big *H*, a big *B*, and a bunch of scribbles. But below that there was another signature. This one was much clearer and read, "Hilda Hillbrook."

Ghost Facts

(ACCORDING TO E, CONT.)

"Hillbrook, Hillbrook," Thelma whispered to herself and furiously flipped through the Riverfish Valley telephone book.

They'd moved the investigation over to Barney Beans. After all, Thelma reasoned, even in—or maybe especially in—life-or-death situations, it's important to eat breakfast.

"Hick, Higgins, Hill, Hillstead … Ugh!!!" She pushed the book across the table in frustration, where it slid into Alexander's anticipating hands. "There's not a single Hillbrook in Riverfish Valley. How is that possible?"

"Well, to be fair, I don't think I've ever even met a Hillbrook. It's a pretty unique name. Also, you told me that the old lady said she was from 'elsewhere,' so it makes perfect sense that she's not listed in the local phone directory. Additionally ... who uses phone books anymore?" Alexander said, not trying to sound like a complete know-it-all but succeeding anyway.

Thelma dropped her head backward and stared up at the white ceiling of the café in annoyance. "A lot of good this does us now. What a disaster," she groaned

"I got a boatload of strawberry pancakes here!" Eugene approached the depressed pair with an upbeat expression and a lot of maple syrup.

"Hey, Eugene," Alexander said, reaching out to grab his stack of hot breakfast.

"Oh little *amigos*, do I have a story for you. That ghost hunt last night? It was out of control!"

Thelma's body stiffened at the thought of a ghost hunt. She'd had enough paranormal experience in the past twenty-four hours. Much more than enough, actually. She decided it was definitely not something to be taken lightly.

"It was crazy," he accentuated the last word and searched their faces for the appropriate reaction. "A one of a kind *experiencia!*" he looked to Thelma for translation but she stayed silent. "OK, something's wrong, that one was basically a freebie. Hey, Thelma Bean, are you OK?" He placed a plate in front of her. The smell of the hot, fluffy, sweet pancakes overcame her sense of complete and utter despondence. She lifted her chin.

"Yeah. Sure," she said, purposefully avoiding eye contact.

"Look me in the eyes, *chica*." Eugene scooted Alexander over and sat opposite Thelma. "You've got something you're not telling me."

Thelma paused. She looked at Alexander, and he nodded as if to give her the go-ahead.

"Listen, Eugene, something bad happened, but it's not normal bad, it's really weird bad, OK?"

Eugene looked worried and lowered his voice. "You got it. It's a slow morning, and I've got Jaclyn helping with the tables. You just tell me what's going on."

"It kind of has to do with … a ghost," Thelma began, staring at her syrupy fork, afraid to meet Eugene's eyes.

Eugene's expression lightened and he took a big breath. "OK, this I can handle! Listen, girl, if you want to talk ghosties, I am your man. You've seen my gear, I'm a believer."

Thelma mustered her confidence and began. "Well, some old lady came into the shop yesterday and sold my dad this small wooden box thing." She pointed to the antique, which sat beside her on the booth. "I knew she was weird, but … anyway." She shook her head to gather her thoughts, "There's a ghost that lives in it, and it sucked my dad into this box last night. He's gone."

Eugene was stunned into silence. He narrowed his eyes and puckered his mouth in thought. "So you're telling me that your daddy, Mr. Henry Bee, is in there?" He pointed at the jewelry box.

"Yes," she took a deep breath. It actually felt really

good to talk to someone else about this, "Yes, that's what I'm telling you."

Eugene sat back in the booth and put his hand to his forehead. He looked a little pale. "Now I know it's not April first, but I gotta ask anyway..."

"It's not a joke, Eugene. And it's definitely not a prank," said Thelma.

Alexander chimed in. "We want to track down the owner of the jewelry box. The, you know, previous owner. We know the lady's name, but we can't find her in the phone book."

"Well, what's her name?" Eugene asked, slowly recovering.

"Hillbrook," Alexander and Thelma said in unison.

Eugene squinted. "Hillbrook, hmm."

Thelma leaned forward in her chair with anticipation.

"Nope. No, never heard the name. Tell you what, though—from what you're telling me here, you've got a very haunted antique."

"No kidding," she said.

"Well, I didn't tell you about the hunt we had last night." Eugene leaned in and spoke quietly, "I don't know if it was a full moon or what, but it seems like the spirits were really out in full force."

"You documented something?" Alexander straightened up, eager for details. Then he caught himself and looked carefully at Thelma, to see if she was upset at his intense interest.

Eugene rubbed the back of his neck and nodded.

"Well, I've been on a lot of investigations with the team. Man, I've been hunting with RVPS for about a year and a half now. Stood in my fair share of creepy rooms with the lights off, is what I'm telling you. I've felt things before. We all have—but nothing like last night."

The story began to pique Thelma's interest. If nothing else, she was desperate for distraction. Constantly thinking about her dad was boring a sick, hurting hole in her chest and she needed relief. She reached for her notebook.

"What, exactly, happened?" Alexander's brow was stitched with intrigue.

"It's hard to explain, except that, well … sometimes our evidence is a little fuzzy," said Eugene. Thelma nodded. A frustration of unorthodox research that was extremely familiar to her because of her mother's unconventional work.

"There's no two ways about it. There's a ghost at Magistrate's Manse," Eugene continued, "He's there. He wants to be heard."

"Did he talk to you, Eugene?" Thelma was scared to ask the question. She got a shiver remembering the lady's buzzing voice from the night before.

"He did, ma'am. He positively did. We got it recorded and it's no 'could've been the wind' EVP. No way."

"I hope your hat worked," Alexander said, eyes wide, "You're recording hat, I mean. Did you get a recording?"

"Started to, but then the thing went dead, just like that," he snapped. Eugene pursed his lips and inhaled deeply through his nose before turning to Thelma.

"I think in some kinda way, this is might be a good thing," he said.

"A good thing?" Thelma's face flushed. She resisted the temptation to fling a strawberry chunk at her friend's head.

Eugene put his hands up, "You're missing my point, Thelma Bean—I think we gotta go back to the Manse and bring your antique."

"Yes!" Alexander sprung up from his seat and grabbed Thelma's hand.

"Thelma, think about it. You've got a haunted item and Eugene has a talkative ghost—this is perfect!"

Thelma had a difficult time imagining how anything about their current situation was perfect. Aside from the strawberry pancakes. Did a ghost problem call for a ghost solution? She didn't know, but it was their only lead.

She stabbed a fresh strawberry with her fork and popped it into her mouth. Chewing, she nodded, "OK. When do we leave?"

COMMUNICATION RECEIVED:

Mr. Thistle

Eugene drove an old gray Pontiac that he called Gary Indiana. It was just before dusk as he, Alexander, and Thelma cruised down the leafy road that connected Riverfish to Cooktown in old Gary. The New England trees were like a box of crayons come to rustling life—orange, red, brown, green, and yellow. Thelma leaned back and watched the trees move by, linking her fingers together over the red backpack on her lap. She felt the geometric edges of the box through the canvas. She wanted to get to the Manse fast, but there was a part of her that also wanted to turn around and go home, bury her head under the quilt on her couch, and pretend like none of this was happening.

Some tourists traveled to the Riverfish area at this time of year solely for the purpose of driving slowly (very slowly) to view the beautiful scenery. Gary Indiana was stuck behind one such leaf peeper and could not accelerate past twenty miles per hour for the entire ride.

They were scheduled to meet the rest of Eugene's RVPS team at 5:00 P.M., but it was nearly half past the hour when they neared the house. Thelma felt a tingle down her back. The property was flanked by evergreens, and the trees kept the house largely hidden from the road. When Gary Indiana pulled onto the narrow drive that led to the main gate, the goliath trees gave way to a clearing and she saw the place.

Dark, pointed gables punctured the twilight sky at uncomfortable angles, turning the pretty crayon-box scenery into the backdrop of a horror movie. The road turned to packed dirt as they cruised up the drive. Eugene parked the car next to a huge rotted stump, and Thelma scooted out of the backseat and swung the red backpack over her shoulder. Eugene led the way up to the main entrance as Thelma and Alexander exchanged nervous looks.

The Manse was much bigger than Thelma had anticipated. Most historical sites in the area were smaller in scale, even government buildings and churches. The Manse was one-of-a-kind. The dark brown wood made deliberate horizontal lines across the face of the house, interrupted by a door so tall and wide that Thelma felt uncomfortable knocking. It seemed that the person who built the place wanted visitors to feel intimidated. It worked.

Just as Eugene was about to grab the iron knocker, the door swung open with a *whoosh*. There stood a young girl with an intensely cross look on her face and a thick blonde braid sprouting like a fountain from the top of her head. She wore black jeans and a matching jacket with a RVPS patch sewn onto the right arm. Both the girl and her jacket were extremely small, and the patch took up most of the space on her sleeve.

"A half hour late, Eugene? Really?" Her mouth puckered in disapproval.

"Sorry, Izzy," Eugene stammered.

"Where's the antique?" she demanded.

Eugene led Alexander and Thelma into the open foyer. As Thelma passed by Izzy, the miniature investigator focused on her backpack and made a grabbing motion causing Thelma to recoil away from her and come to quick judgment about this girl's attitude problem. When she established a decent buffer zone between her and the overzealous blondie, Thelma pulled the box out of her backpack and hugged it to her chest.

"This is Izzy." Eugene put a patient hand on the girl's shoulder. "She's not very good at introductions. Are you, miss?"

"Sorry," she said, half rolling her eyes. "My name is Izzy Finkle, and I'm a paranormal investigator."

"Junior," Eugene corrected.

"Fine. Junior paranormal investigator. Also, the resident expert on magic and the occult. My cousin

Ricky is the founder of RVPS, so I've basically been hunting ghosts my whole
life."

"So, what? For, like, nine years?"
Thelma scoffed.

"Twelve, actually. I'm short for my
age." Izzy put one hand on her already
jutted-out hip.

This had to be a joke. This girl with
her black fingernails and weirdo
hair seemed to be under the impression that she could boss everyone around. Pathetic. Thelma
rolled her eyes and laughed
quietly, looking to Alexander
for commiseration. What
she saw instead was
Alexander, her best

friend in the entire universe, looking at Izzy Finkle like she was some kind of movie star. His eyes were as wide as saucers as he introduced himself and shook her hand.

"Hi, Izzy, I'm Alexander Oldtree. Thanks so much for having us"

"Alexander! Don't be weird. What's wrong with you?" Thelma hissed in a whisper that was much louder than she anticipated. It was a voice she was immediately a little embarrassed by.

His light brown skin turned a shade of eggplant and he lowered his head. It seemed like Thelma would not be the only one to benefit from a face unreddener.

"I'm just excited for the investigation," he mumbled, shooting Thelma a hurt look.

Izzy led Eugene, Thelma, and the still-embarrassed Alexander up a flight of creaky stairs and into a wide hallway lined with plush Victorian chairs and doilied coffee tables. Golden lamplight gave the place a dreamlike feeling, like they were in another time alto-gether.

At the end of the hallway, two people stood outside a bedroom, one man and one woman. The man was a short, chubby guy with kinky red hair and a very large pair of glasses. This was Ricky.

"Hey, you guys! I'm so glad you made it!" Ricky bounded over to them like a puppy. "You must be Thelma," he continued. His expression sobered once he realized maybe he was acting a little too peppy considering the circumstances.

The woman had followed Ricky more slowly. She was Menkin Jones. She had a pronounced nose, light brown hair, and an expression that could be described as "muted terror" on her face. She attempted to smile and wave a casual hello, but was clearly out of her ele-ment.

"Thelma," Ricky said, "I am so sorry for your ordeal. Eugene filled us in on everything. If there's any way that RVPS can help in this difficult time, you just let us know." He had very kind eyes and a high, crackly voice. He was nothing at all like his cousin. Thelma liked him.

"Um, thanks," Thelma stammered.

"Ricky, examine the antique," Izzy insisted. "She won't let me touch it."

"And I'm sure you didn't try to mug her as soon as she got here, did you?" Ricky asked.

Menkin Jones smiled at Ricky's joke.

"Get a life, Menkin." Izzy snapped.

Ricky rolled his eyes and turned to Thelma.

"I'm sorry, Thelma. I know your father is, well, potentially in that box you've got there, but may I examine it before we take it to the bedchamber?" He motioned to the closed door down the hall, "That's where we recorded all the activity last night."

"Since you asked so nicely," Thelma said, glaring at Izzy, "then yes, of course you can."

Ricky took the jewelry box, handling it with extreme gentleness, running his hands around its surface. He tried to simply pull open the tiny inter-locked brass hands.

"Well, it's definitely locked." He looked up from his investigation.

"Obviously," Izzy added. "We need to open it."

Thelma and Alexander spoke at the same time.

"Totally," said Alexander.

"Obviously," snorted Thelma.

Thelma scowled at Alexander and felt her blood start to boil again. *10 Mississippi, 9 Mississippi, 8 Mississippi …*

Eugene shifted nervously. "Do you think we're ready to head in?"

"Hah. OK. I'm just gonna …" Menkin Jones grimaced and gestured to the hallway. She wasn't coming in, that's for sure. Thelma wondered if she was going to have a heart attack just being inside the house. A fraidy-cat ghost hunter? That was a peculiar thing.

Ricky nodded toward Menkin kindly, and the rest

of the group headed toward the end of the hall and the room where the ghost resided. Thelma's heart pounded, and she held the box tightly. Ricky opened the door and walked inside. He was followed by Eugene, Alexander, Izzy, and finally, in back, Thelma.

A few candles flickered dimly, illuminating the chamber. Thelma scanned the room. Beads of sweat began to form on her forehead despite the cool temperature. High ceiling, two large windows that faced the sunset garden, a large bed in the middle of the room, and a few bookcases. It looked normal enough.

Since Eugene's microphone hat had shorted out, he, Izzy, and Ricky clutched small black audio recorders. Thelma tightened her hold on the box even more.

"Mr. Thistle," Ricky directed his calm voice into the darkness, "We have come here to speak with you again."

Silence. Thelma wiped her forehead with the sleeve of her shirt.

"Well?" she asked in a whisper.

"Be patient, Thelma Bean," Eugene said softly.

"Mr. Thistle, you spoke with us last night. We'd like to speak with you again. Are you here?"

Silence.

Thelma thought she could feel a cold pressure on her shoulder, but she ignored it. She got a sinking feeling in her heart. While the idea of contacting another spirit 100 percent totally terrified her, she hadn't even entertained the idea of this not working. It had to work. There was no plan B. Her heart beat hard.

"Mr. Thistle," Ricky continued calmly ...

"Are you here?" Thelma yelled—everyone jumped, taken off guard by her outburst.

"If you're here I need to talk to you right now, OK? It's really important!" Her emotions intensified. She heard her blood pumping in her ears and a panicky feeling trickled through her body. Soon it became less of a trickle and more like a pulsing. A burning. She'd make that spirit talk. She concentrated so hard on him. With one hand she gripped her opal necklace.

"Thelma, hold still." In the candlelight she saw Alexander's face—his expression was extremely serious.

"What's wrong with her?" Izzy asked Ricky, "Why does she look like that?" Then with exasperation, "Did anyone even bring a video camera?"

Why did she look like what? wondered Thelma. She looked down at her arm and she saw what they'd all seen, she was kind of ... glowing.

"You ... burn."

The candles extinguished at once.

The voice that spoke those words did not belong to Eugene, Ricky, Izzy, or Alexander. It was a man's voice, a raw voice, and it sounded like it was coming through the far wall, from another room.

Thelma tried to hold still. Yes, she was burning, but it didn't hurt at all. If anything, it felt good. It felt powerful. It gave her courage.

"Is that you, Mr. Thistle?" she asked.

"You ... witch?" asked the voice. The spaces

between his words didn't sound completely empty. Like there were other voices too, whispering over each other in a crisscross pattern. Incomprehensible. Mr. Thistle's rose above the scratchy din with terrible clarity.

Izzy's jaw nearly dropped to the floor. Ricky put his arm around her protectively, but still held out the recorder.

"Witch?" she asked.

"Why ... summon ... me ... witch?"

Thelma gathered her wits and took a deep breath. The heat in her blood made her feel bold.

"My father is in here. He was taken." She held the box out. A cold gust blew past her cheek and she jumped, nearly dropping the box. She felt a cooling through her body as the burning subsided.

Silence returned to the room. Everyone's gaze focused on Thelma. She could feel their eyes. They waited for a response for a few moments before Alexander went over to the far wall and touched it, looking for some kind of explanation. He ran his hands along the bumpy old wallpaper. Eugene shook out his arms like he was limbering up before a gymnastic meet. Izzy and Ricky began arguing quietly about whose responsibility it was to bring the video camera.

"What, is that it?" Thelma yelled. They all looked back at her.

"I think he's gone," said Alexander.

"No!" she boomed. "Mr. Thistle, return! Come back here now!" The warm feeling returned to her body.

The team fell silent. That's when the floor started to rumble.

"Yes ..." Izzy hissed under her breath, "It's happening."

Thelma gasped as she felt, as clearly as she'd ever felt anything in her life, two cold, invisible hands grip her own. She no longer had control of her own hands' movements.

"Al—" she tried calling for her best friend, but terror stole her voice. Her hands turned the box upside down and felt the wood along the burned-in inscription. Her fingers found a subtle notch in the wood and pulled with more strength than she would have had alone. A large key fell on to the matted carpet next to her sneakers.

She whispered, "OK ... OK ... thank you ..."

Izzy screamed, and the recorder she held shot from her hand and landed on the floor next to the key. The rewind button pressed down by itself, followed by play.

The audio recording played a scratchy voice:

"Do not open. Do not open. Do not open. Do not open. Do not open. Do not open. Do not open." A click. End of tape.

The entire investigating team, along with Thelma and Alexander, stood in a circle around the box in the front yard of Magistrate's Manse.

"Maybe we should just hand it over to the police?" Menkin offered with an embarrassed shuffle.

"Menkin, as I always tell you, we are a volunteer organization," Izzy said. "If you don't want to be involved in this investigation anymore, you are invited to take a hike."

"We carpooled here," Menkin mumbled under her breath, bringing her hand up to her temple as though her head ached.

"OK," said Ricky, placing a hand on Menkin's shoulder. "What is our plan?"

"We open the box!" Thelma couldn't believe there was even a discussion. This was after all, a matter of life and, well, she hoped it wasn't a matter of life and death. But she knew her dad was stuck in some place that even a ghost was afraid of.

"She's right," said Alexander. "We've got to open it up. Mr. Bee is in there, and we've got to get him out. It's a … it's a moral imperative." He nodded meaningfully at Thelma. She exhaled. At least Alexander was still on her side.

"OK, OK! Listen, people," Eugene finally piped up. "This is a serious piece of business. Ricky, I think this is the biggest case RVPS has ever seen." Ricky nodded in agreement as Eugene continued. "The only smart thing to do right now is sleep on it."

Thelma groaned.

"You hear me, *chica*?"

"How is that the only smart thing to do?" she asked

with less passion in her voice than she intended. She suddenly felt drained of energy.

"It's late. We are tired. And this is dangerous stuff. Thelma Bean, I don't want to take chances with your safety. OK, girl?"

"Yeah," she sighed and put her hands up to her forehead in exasperation.

Ricky, Menkin, and Eugene huddled up and talked in hushed voices while Alexander listened intently. Thelma's body felt completely exhausted. She sat on the chilly ground.

Even though she understood Eugene's point, she couldn't help feeling like no one, not even her best friend, really understood what she was going through. What was her dad experiencing? The thought scared Thelma terribly. She was grateful that she had a team helping to rescue her dad, but this wasn't just a case or an investigation for her—it was the very real possibility of losing one of the most important people in the world. She glanced at the box and her heart broke again. It had been breaking all day.

"Hey," Izzy whispered, plopping herself down on the ground next to her.

"What?" Thelma growled.

"You ever do that before?"

"What?" Thelma knew what.

"You know what."

"No, I guess that was Mr. Thistle."

"Absolutely insane. What did that feel like?"

Alexander walked over right in time to save her from any further conversation with Izzy, who was having the charming effect that the hard side of Velcro has on an open wound.

"Gotta go," he said. "We'll see you tomorrow I think, Izzy. Thanks for everything."

Thelma barfed a thousand internal barfs.

"OK," Izzy called after Thelma as she walked back toward Eugene's car, "Whatever. Later, then."

"You OK?" Alexander asked Thelma.

"I don't know," she said.

"The ... um ..."

"Glowing." She finished his sentence for him, "I don't know, I can't explain it. And he called me a witch, which doesn't make any sense at all."

"I didn't like it, you know?" his expression was crumpled, "It felt dangerous ... or something."

"It didn't hurt or anything," Thelma swung the red backpack around to her front as they reached Gary Indiana, "I'll just add it to the list of ghost observations. It's getting to be a long list ..."

Alexander nodded and climbed into the backseat.

"You're OK," he said. "Not a witch."

She forced a laugh that she didn't really feel.

"If you say so."

Izzy:
Skilled Home Invader

(SUBSTANTIATED)

There was no sleep for Thelma that chilly night. She clutched her opal necklace as she lay awake, staring alternately at the ceiling, the doorway, and Alexander, who snoozed on the floor of her room. His gentle, hoarse breathing was the only thing keeping her tethered to reality. Thank goodness for his over-achieving sisters and their out-of-town championship games. Otherwise the whole business of a no-parents sleepover might have been tricky.

She wanted to take deep breaths and fill up her whole body, like the trick her father had taught her to help fall asleep.

"Breathe in through your nose," he'd instructed, "and take the air all the way down to your toes. Now fill your toes up with that air like you're a balloon…"

Thelma's toes were not like balloons filling

up at all. They were just toes. Toes stuck to a body that did not want to relax, did not want to breathe deep, and most certainly did not want to sleep.

Her mind began to wander. The term "daddy's girl" was silly. It sounded like the kind of girl who wore fancy dresses or collected dolls or lip gloss or other useless stuff. It was a term you might see scrawled on one of Jenny Sullivan's t-shirts in loopy writing. Thelma didn't want to be a "daddy's girl," she just really loved her dad. Whether it was debating whether there was life on Mars, creating blueprints for backyard greenhouses, or just listening intently to her while she explained the horror of middle school lockers, he was always there.

Thelma loved both of her parents so much, but ever since that antique showed up in her life, she began to understand how different her relationships with her two parents were. Mom traveled the world, Dad stayed home. Mom told wild stories of faraway places. But Dad had been the one who tucked her in at night and wiped away her tears. He made her feel strong and safe.

She had always felt free to dream of dangerous adventures like Mary Bee's because deep down inside Thelma always knew that she was protected, and that if there ever were any real monsters, Henry would scare them away. But now, everything was different. There was no map to guide her way, no safety net to catch her if she fell. She only had herself now, and she wondered if that was enough. And if it wasn't enough, what then? The swirling sadness in her stomach was a black hole and it was eating her up.

Thump.

Thelma bolted upright. There was a noise downstairs, it sounded like it came from the kitchen. Someone was trying to come in through the window.

"Alexander!" she said, trying to whisper and achieve maximum volume at the same time. It sounded like a cat with a hairball problem. She reached her foot down and pushed on his shoulder. "Alexander!"

"What is it, Thelma? Geez … it's the middle of the night."

Then another noise from the kitchen, this time a banging, jolted him out of his sleepy state. He looked at Thelma with wide eyes. She climbed down from her bed and searched the room for possible weapons, wishing she'd been successful in acquiring those grappling hooks last month.

She tiptoed over to the corner where she kept a baseball bat. It had only ever been used in her fifth-grade art installation project "Wooden Robots: An Almost-Functional Option." She picked it up, wondering if she'd have the wherewithal to actually whack someone with it. Alexander looked around for a weapon and could find nothing more threatening than a thickish book, so he grabbed that and held it over his head. The two of them walked very, very quietly toward the door. They'd have to make it all the way downstairs undetected.

Suddenly the lights flicked on. In the threshold of the bedroom stood a tiny twelve-year-old with black fingernails and a smirk on her face. Izzy.

"Hope I didn't wake you up."

Both Thelma and Alexander exhaled with tremendous relief.

"What do you think you're doing?" Thelma asked, putting her bat back in the corner. "You can't just break into people's houses, you know. It's insane. And rude."

"Well, apparently I can actually break into people's houses. Especially when they leave the windows unlocked."

Alexander chuckled at Izzy's weak attempt at a joke, and any relief at seeing her fell away from Thelma immediately.

"We probably should have secured the house. You're right," he said.

"You didn't answer my first question," Thelma snapped. "What are you doing here?"

"Do you want some tea or something?" Alexander offered.

"Yeah, that would be great," Izzy replied.

Thelma pushed past Izzy and down the stairs. "Great," she grumbled. "Everyone just make yourselves at home."

Izzy, Alexander, and Thelma sat around the dining room table, with a plate of cookies and steaming cups of Earl Grey, which Dad always kept in stock, each with milk and sugar. Chewing on her lip, Thelma eyed the box that sat in the corner of the room. Eugene had wanted to take it home with him, or back to the shop, but Thelma refused, so it was spending the night in her house.

"I was thinking about your dad," Izzy said.

"Huh?"

"You asked me before, why I came over. I was thinking about your dad. Actually, I was thinking about my dad. And my mom."

"I don't get it." Thelma warmed her hands on her mug.

"Something bad happened to them?" Alexander asked.

"Yeah. When I was little."

"What was it?" Thelma asked.

"I mean, if you don't mind talking about it," Alexander added with a nervous glance at Thelma.

"Um, yeah. I don't know. It was an accident, basically. I was four, and we were crossing the street. They were ahead, and me and Ricky and my aunt Lorraine were behind them. There was a car that just came out of nowhere …" Izzy trailed off a little bit and took a sip of her tea. "You get it."

Thelma got it. She felt a guilty pit inside her stomach. Or maybe it wasn't guilt, but empathy. The mere possibility of losing her dad had turned her inside out—she couldn't imagine the pain of losing both her parents.

"I'm sorry. That must have been so terrible," she said.

"I don't know what to say. I'm sorry." Alexander looked down at his mug.

"It was a long time ago." Izzy forced a little smile. "But it still hurts. Obviously."

"Is that why you started with the … um …"

"Paranormal stuff?" Izzy finished Thelma's question. "Yeah, it is. I started off because I wanted to talk to my parents again. I wanted to connect with them and tell them that I love them and miss them and all that."

"Were you ever able to?" Alexander asked.

"No. I guess it's not supposed to work that way, maybe. But I still love learning about the field. And every time we meet a ghost I think, maybe that guy knows my parents." She exhaled quietly. "That's dumb, I know, but it's kind of my way of dealing, I guess. There's just one thing that I have never been able to get over."

"What is it?" asked Thelma.

"The car. I mean, I was really young, but I saw the car and they didn't. And I should have, you know, yelled out or something, but it happened too fast and then they were just … gone."

She looked at Thelma. "Listen, you have to go get your dad." Izzy's eyes glistened. "You might be able to save him, and if there's any chance in the world you can, you have to. That's why I came here tonight. Because I have a feeling, a really strong one, that every minute he's in there, he gets further away from us. We've got to do something tonight."

The heaviness moved up from Thelma's stomach to her throat, and she pursed her lips tight to keep back the tears. Izzy reached across the table and grabbed her hand. Now Thelma drew in a big breath, all the way down to her toes. She filled them up like balloons and tried hard to exhale it all out. All of the scared feeling, all of the anger, all of the feeling bad for herself, she tried hard to let it out.

Izzy was right. If there was any chance in the whole wide world that she could save her dad, she had to try. And she didn't want to wait a second longer.

"So." Thelma stood up from her chair. "How do we do this?"

Izzy walked over to the box, grabbed it, and placed it in the middle of the table. Then Alexander reached out and turned it on its side. He picked up the key. It was plain and dark and he turned it around in his hands. He disappeared momentarily into the kitchen, and emerged with a Taco Heaven magnet from Thelma's refrigerator. They observed as it stuck to the key.

"Iron, I think," he concluded.

"Are you ready, Thelma?" Izzy looked nervous even though she tried to make her voice sound brave.

"Now?" Her heart raced a little, "I'll probably need shoes," Thelma said as she looked down at her bare feet.

"So, you think it's going to like … suck you in?" Izzy asked.

"Seems like that's what this thing does," Thelma replied, squinting at the box.

"What about food?" Alexander's face suddenly furrowed with worry. "And a coat, maybe? A map, for sure." He began to pace around the room.

Thelma grabbed her sneakers and sat down to tie them tight. "A map of what? I don't think it's just, like, Rhode Island in there. A map won't help," she said.

"This will." Izzy touched the necklace around Thelma's neck. The opal.

"What do you mean?" Thelma asked, touching the stone.

"It's hard to explain, and it might come from spending so much time trying to communicate with the other side, but … I can feel things sometimes."

"Feel things? Like psychic stuff?"

"I guess. I don't know, still kind of figuring it out. But, for some reason I know that necklace is special. I have a feeling that it's going to protect you," said Izzy.

A light bulb went off in Thelma's brain.

"The ghost, on the night she came she was kind of … reaching for it."

"Return!" said Alexander, "That's what the ghost said, right?"

"Details that would have been helpful," Izzy's looked from Thelma to Alexander with the peeved expression of someone who has been left out of the loop.

Alexander ignored Izzy and grabbed Thelma's shoulder, "Of course! A ghost emerges from a jewelry box, points to your necklace and says, 'return.' She obviously wants the necklace! Your mom said it was old, right?"

"Yeah, I mean, I think so," Thelma tried her hardest to remember what her mom had said when she gave it to her. Mom had made a big deal about it, that's for sure. She said it was special—so yeah. It probably was a very old, valuable thing.

"OK, this is the plan. Get in there, trade your necklace for your dad, and get back out."

The three of them stood silently contemplating the plan for a moment.

"Yeah, get back out," Izzy said with a sober look. Alexander's gaze fell to his feet.

"OK," Thelma clutched the necklace. The thought of giving it away made her heart sink. She was surprised at how much sorrow she felt when she thought of being parted from the little thing. It was just a necklace.

It was still inky dark outside, and the clock said 4:35 A.M. Now was as good a time as any. Thelma steadied herself, trying to ignore the frantic bumping of her heart against her ribcage. With a look of excruciating anxiety on his face, Alexander handed her the key. He stepped away from her for a moment but rushed toward Thelma again, wrapping his arms around her so tight that she felt smothered.

"Thelma, be very careful, please!" He finally let go, and she caught her breath.

"I will, Alexander. Thanks." She smiled. Then, turning to Izzy, she said, "Thank you too, Izzy."

"You better go." Izzy nodded.

Thelma thought of her mother, a woman who had discovered the Filipino dragonsnake, a woman who once fought a polar bear using only her winter hat, a woman who right at that very moment was traversing the Appalachian Trail on a search for a legendary monster at least three times her size. Thelma was Mary Goosefoot Bee's daughter. And she was bound on a unique kind of adventure—she was heading into a different kind of uncharted territory.

Thelma nodded to her friends and stepped up to the jewelry box. Her shaking hand pushed the key into the keyhole and turned. First, she felt the familiar click of a releasing lock. Then she felt the wind.

Uncharted Territory

CHARTED

The world around Thelma lost its shape. It was as though everything in the room—the table, the windows, even Alexander and Izzy—were made of sand. There were bits of light that flickered like electrical shocks—they only lasted split seconds. Thelma raised her arms up to protect her face as a wind swept through, eroding all of it. She closed her eyes tightly and when she opened them there was nothing around her but dust and darkness.

The transition had an immediate, overwhelmingly depressing effect on her. This world was endlessly bleak. However, her inner scientist couldn't help but be intrigued and excited. Thelma was desperate to document what was happening. Her body must be breaking down into atomic particles and then somehow reassembling. It was impossible, but it was happening. What would this look like under a microscope? Then everything stopped shifting and settled into a gray that was very near to black.

She looked around frantically for some kind of geographical indication of where she was, but there was nothing. She did feel like she was outside. Through her shoes she could sense that the ground she stood on was cold, maybe even frozen, and the air was dusty and frigid. Alexander had been right about the coat, Thelma thought to herself as she grabbed onto her own arms and rubbed furiously to feel some kind of warmth.

She bent down and touched the dusty ground. She tried to collect some of the dust to put in her pocket for later examination, but it was so fine and the atmosphere so disorienting, she couldn't be certain that she actually got any. Thelma thought of her backyard and the soil there. It was cool, but also moist and teeming with life. You could feel connectivity when you put your hands on the earth by the river. This dirt here was different. It was dead. There was a palpable absence of life, of hope.

"Hello?" she yelled, but no one answered. "Dad?" She couldn't see much of anything. It was then she started to get a sensation in her stomach. A dull ache, similar to hunger but heavier. She should have listened to Alexander on all preparation accounts. But, hunger didn't really make sense. She'd just snacked on a few cookies and tea—and she wasn't even hungry before she ate those. This was a strange place, and Thelma didn't like it one bit. It filled her with a painful emptiness.

She had to do something, so she walked forward, shouting every few minutes. There was no way to know if she was going north or south, or if this place had any direction at all. Every now and then Thelma would reach up and touch the necklace. It was warm, even here, and when she concentrated on that warm feeling, she felt more in control. Maybe Izzy was right.

The walk lasted for what seemed like hours. Once, Thelma tried to sit down and rest, but the cold soil sent such a chill through her whole body that she stood up again and kept going. Every so often she heard something like a scream, but it came from too far away to know for sure. Doubts flooded her mind. She thought of her mother returning home to find not only her husband but also her daughter missing. Suddenly the whole expedition seemed so foolish.

Why did she do this alone? Where was her father? Thelma wiped the dust off of her face and accidentally inhaled some of the particles. She coughed so hard that she almost threw up. She felt her lungs burn, and then fell to her knees. She screamed in anger and pounded on the freezing soil.

She yelled again and again, pounding the ground until there was no energy left in her arms or voice or heart. She remembered Mr. Thistle's warning. A place so terrible even a ghost would stay away, and yet here she was. The cold trickled up her legs and arms like skeleton fingers. If she stopped moving, this was the end. She'd read a story once about some guy freezing to death in the forest, how he just fell asleep and that was that. A dark thought crept into Thelma's imagination. Maybe she could let go and fall asleep. A cold, long sleep would be better than this. Anything would. But then she would fail her family and her friends and never see another sunny day in Riverfish.

Sorrow weaved around her like a spider web. She closed her eyes against the wind and tried to get a hold of herself. She counted, up this time, 1 *Mississippi*, 2 *Mississippi* … When Thelma got to 10, she opened her eyes. What she saw startled her nearly to death. A woman. She was wearing a white dress.

In appearance though, this woman wasn't really that scary. In fact, she was quite beautiful, even wreathed in the gray-black wind. The sadness that Thelma felt inside, all the hunger, the cold, and the hopelessness, she saw it all reflected on this person's face.

On further examination, she wasn't yet a woman at all. She was a girl—probably sixteen or seventeen years old. The girl stood only a few steps in front of Thelma, and she watched as Thelma dragged herself off the cold ground. The girl waved for Thelma to follow, so she did. They walked a short distance and came to an enormous tree with tar-black bark.

The girl in the white dress took both of her delicate

hands and pushed on a large knot in the trunk. As she did, a doorway appeared. Both girls ducked through the low opening, and soon Thelma found herself in a strange, small room. There were two chairs, one table, and a dim wax candle that illuminated the space with a small light. The girl sat in one of the chairs and gestured to Thelma to sit across from her.

By the light of the dim candle, Thelma was better able to study the girl's face. There was something oddly familiar in her expression, her large light eyes, her small chin, but it was impossible to pinpoint. Thelma coughed as she tried to speak. There was still some dust in her throat.

"Please," she began, "please tell me where my father is."

The girl looked down at her hands. "He is here."

"Here, in this house?"

"No. Not precisely. But he is here."

"You ... you brought him here."

"Yes."

"Is he ..."

"He's alive," said the girl with a peculiar sharpness.

Thelma sighed in relief. She turned to the girl. She knew she should be angry, that she should yell and demand her father's return. But looking at the girl's face, Thelma was only overwhelmed by sadness and confusion.

"I don't understand. Who are you?"

"My name is Annabelle," the girl said, and breathed deeply. "I am sorry. I have caused you pain and worry."

"I just want my dad back. Please, Annabelle. You," Thelma paused because the words were hard, "You can have the necklace. I know you want it. Just, I need my dad."

Annabelle's eyes showed a glimmer of light. "The necklace is yours, Thelma. I do not wish to steal it from you."

"But, you said …"

"You must help me."

"How do you know my name? I don't understand this place. Where are we?" asked Thelma.

"I've seen you, and I know you. But as for where we are, that I do not know."

"But don't you live here?" Thelma's confusion only grew as they continued to talk.

"One doesn't live here. Here one is kept from life. And from death. I have been here for many years. There is much that you need to understand."

"I came here to get my dad, Annabelle. He doesn't belong here—I've got to get him home."

"Home." Annabelle sighed. "I want to go home too."

Thelma steadied herself. The rumbling in her stomach wouldn't stop. "Where is he?"

Annabelle stood up, steel in her voice. "You may not have him yet. Not until you help me. I'm sorry."

Thelma leaned back in her creaky seat.

"This isn't fair," she said.

"No." Annabelle took her seat. "Not fair in the least," she looked at Thelma with intensity. "But you have no choice."

This really was a hideous place. It made Thelma's bones ache with chill. It made her stomach growl with painful hunger. Had Dad spent days here? Had Annabelle spent years? Thelma could think of no other plan. Annabelle was her only hope of saving her dad and going back home.

"OK," Thelma said.

Annabelle took a deep breath and began.

Ghost Facts

(ACCORDING TO GHOST)

"I grew up in a small village called Marlomet," Annabelle began. "Father owned a lumber mill, and we were a modest family, with modest means." Annabelle stopped talking. She looked down at her hands and stayed very quiet for a moment.

"So, what happened? What do I need to do to get my dad?" Thelma asked, desperate to keep things on track.

"Childhood cannot last forever, though one might wish it so." Annabelle lowered her chin. There was some unspoken meaning in these words, but Thelma didn't ask any questions. Annabelle continued, "I will tell you the story of a man named Zachariah Understone. Then you will understand what you must do."

"Fine." Thelma didn't see another way around it.

"Zachariah Understone did business with my father. He had no relations and tremendous wealth. He also had a strange and cold demeanor and a cruel sensibility. When he walked into a room, I felt a cold chill inside my bones. He made frequent visits. My father disliked him terribly, but he was a wealthy customer, so we treated him with respect."

"Sounds terrible."

"Most thought he was terrible indeed. People in town would speak of this man in whispers. There was talk that he practiced dark arts. Some even said that he kept a demon living with him, whom he locked under the floorboards in his house."

"That's nuts." The thought made Thelma shiver.

Annabelle continued, "Stories from town gossips, or so I thought. But then, on my sixteenth birthday, he asked my father if he could have me for his wife."

"Sixteen?"

"Yes. My family refused. They told him that I would have my own choice of whom to marry once I was of age."

"Well, good," said Thelma, dust still in her throat.

"He offered us wealth. But they wouldn't sell me away, and for that I will always be grateful. They wanted me to find my own true love."

"Did you?" Thelma leaned forward, studying the girl's sad, pretty expression.

"Yes," she smiled. "I met my dear Jonathan one day in June and by August we set a date to wed. But after our engagement, I was paid a visit." Annabelle's eyes fixed on some faraway place. She hugged her arms to her chest.

"I was walking down the road and it was evening. Someone grabbed me and a familiar chill seized my body. It was Mr. Understone."

"Oh no," Thelma gasped.

"He took my arm in his as though he was escorting me home, but instead he pulled me into a dark corner. I was terrified. His skin was waxy and white, his hair black as oil. He told me I was a special, and that I had a light inside of me. He had always favored me above all others.

"Mr. Understone reached inside his coat and pulled out a ring. It was gold, I remember, with a great red gemstone set in the middle. He asked me to be his wife. He told me he could give me many more jewels like this."

"This story is creeping me out," said Thelma.

"I was Jonathan's bride to be, and I told him that. His face twisted and darkened into something that barely looked human.

"'You refuse me?' he growled between his teeth. 'After all the years I've waited for you?' He moved his hands to my neck and he gripped hard. I felt the world spin in confusion." Annabelle paused.

"What? What happened?"

"It may be difficult for you to understand what happened next. I … I became so frightened for my life, and so angry, that I snapped into reality, into the moment. There was an electricity inside me that I'd never felt before. Buzzing in my arms, in my torso, and down my legs. Like I was made of lightning," she glanced at Thelma with a spark in her eyes, like she was searching for recognition.

"He was so much stronger than I, but when I … I willed this electricity to push him back, it did. I did."

Thelma remembered Magistrate's Manse. She had felt so warm, not electricity, but fire. It was not hard for her to understand what had happened to Annabelle at all.

Annabelle continued, "His face was so strange. It looked furious, and then sad. I thought I heard him weeping then, but maybe I was hallucinating. He backed away. He let me go. I was so exhausted from the struggle that I fell to the ground.

"I awoke the next morning in my home with Mother, Father, my sister, Margaret, and Jonathan all by my side. Once I explained what had happened, Jonathan and my father left in a rage to find Mr. Understone, but they never did. His house was well outside of Marlomet, deep in the marshes. When they reached his cottage, there was no sign of the man. No one ever saw him again.

"So he ran away and left you alone?" asked Thelma.

"So we thought," Annabelle said. "We went back about the business of planning the wedding. Those were wonderful days, choosing the food we would prepare, the ribbons we'd hang, the lace for—" Annabelle's voice cracked with emotion, and she put her hands up to her face.

"What's wrong?" Thelma asked. "The lace for what?"

"For this." Annabelle frowned and lifted the skirt of her dress. "For my wedding dress."

Thelma grimaced. It wasn't so different than the one her mother wore on her wedding day. The one in the photo that Annabelle smashed to pieces.

"On my wedding day, I noticed a red ribbon wrapped around a jewelry box. There was a piece of parchment tied to it." Annabelle nodded solemnly when she saw the dread in Thelma's eyes. "Just moments before the ceremony, I read the letter. Understone asked forgiveness and wished me well. And asked if I would please accept this small gift as a token of his everlasting affection for me. I turned the key and opened the box."

"Then?" Thelma cringed—she already knew how this story would end.

"Then everything fell away. I found myself here. If I could not be his, I would not belong to anyone else. There was deep evil in Zachariah Understone's heart. He bewitched this box to keep me forever."

"Was he some kind of wizard ... or something?"

"Only a very powerful and dark magic could conjure this prison."

Thelma was distracted by her roaring stomach. "Annabelle, do you feel ..." Thelma struggled for the right words.

"Empty? Yes. I've felt that for years. It never goes away. It grows and grows." She looked at Thelma, who was hunched over in her chair. "Your bones ache. I feel that too. This is a place without comfort or happiness."

"But I don't understand. You showed up at my house. You must be able to travel out of here sometimes."

Annabelle studied Thelma's face. Her eyes suddenly looked as though they could smile. "Yes. It's you," Annabelle said. "I think that you gave me the strength to transport—though just for a short time. And it was only my shadow that was able to push through."

"Wait ... me? How?"

"I knew."

"Knew what?"

"You are my kin."

"What?"

"My sister, Margaret, went on to marry and have a little girl. Her name was Adeline. Adeline would be your grandmother six generations back."

"Seriously?" Thelma was trying desperately to keep up, "Wait, how do you even know that about your sister? Like, how do you know what happened to her after you disappeared"

"Like I said before, my kin." She looked meaningfully at her young ancestor. "Thelma, when the women in our family join together, we can do impossible things. Sometimes we can even bend worlds. Break magic."

That was maybe too much for Thelma to digest, but she didn't know what else to do besides nod.

Annabelle continued, "Margaret took the box into her home, and I found a way to visit her in her dreams. That small joy was taken away from me eventually too."

"So, you are kind of, like, my aunt?"

"Yes, I knew it when you could feel my presence the first time you picked up the box. I felt connected to you. And now I can tell that much by just looking at you. You've got the eyes of a Dixby girl." Thelma's blue eyes had always made her feel connected to her mom. Now she knew why Annabelle looked familiar.

"And ..." She smiled gently, eyeing Thelma's necklace. "You have some of our other, much stronger traits. You haven't yet discovered your light, but it burns very brightly inside you." She paused and her voice hardened. She exhaled sharply and focused her eyes on Thelma with cold concentration. "That is why I think you are strong enough to help me."

"Help you ..." Thelma had so many unanswered questions.

Annabelle continued, almost to herself, "It could not have been coincidence, I know. I fear by whose design, that I find myself in your father's shop two days before ..."

"Before what?"

Annabelle chose her words carefully. "I've been imprisoned in this chest for two hundred years as of tomorrow. It is time."

"What do you want me to do?" Thelma asked.

"You must return this wedding gift."

"Return? Oh. Return. The gift. That explains why you kept saying that."

"Yes. I frightened you, and I apologize. I could barely keep my body intact, never mind my words. It was a wraith. My shadow self."

"OK," said Thelma, but remembering the evening, she added, "That was terrible. And my house is a disaster," Thelma said.

Annabelle nodded. "My energy, my rage, it all became confused. I lost control. It was such chaos, I nearly forgot why I was there,"

"To steal my father." There was an accusation in Thelma's voice.

Annabelle stood and stepped toward her suddenly, her words escaped in an angry hiss, "I must be freed!"

Thelma gasped at the sudden turn and grabbed her necklace.

Annabelle's eyes darkened. "I must leave this place. My very soul grows black. I can feel the corners of my being sharpen and twist into ... into something terrible. What you saw in your house, that terrible shadow, that is my future if I remain here."

"So, we return the box," said Thelma.

"You do."

"Understone, though. Isn't he dead?" asked Thelma.

Annabelle's look transformed into something Thelma could not translate. "The inscription on the chest will explain it to you." Annabelle's expression softened again. "Thelma, there will be danger. Remember what I told you about your light. About our strength."

The darkness started to flicker and then intensify around them.

"You must go now, Thelma."

"But my dad …"

"He may not leave until you have completed this task." Annabelle walked over and put her icy hand on Thelma's collarbone. She hadn't noticed it before, but Annabelle wore a very thin silver ring on the index finger of her right hand. When the metal of the ring came in contact with the opal around her neck, Thelma felt a powerful electric buzzing and then warmth emanating from her necklace. She grabbed onto it with two hands.

Annabelle's face and body became dark and dusty as the small room faded away. Thelma had so many more questions that she needed answered, but she was being pushed and pulled—out of one world and into another. Her knees buckled as all the strength washed out of her body.

Research and Translation

"Thelma!" Alexander's hair looked weird, like it was hanging in front of his face.

"Thelma! Can you hear us?"

Thelma rubbed her eyes and blinked a few times. She slowly came to the realization that she was lying on the floor.

"She's opening her eyes. Do you think she can hear us?" Izzy whispered.

"Yeah! I can hear you." Thelma sat up and looked around. Alexander rushed over and put his arm around her.

"Thelma! That was crazy—just crazy! You—you, like, turned into smoke or something. We were scared out of our minds!"

"I've never seen anything like that before. Never. And I've seen some crazy stuff." Izzy got down on her knees and touched Thelma's hair. "You're back—you feel like a normal person. Are you still a normal person? This is incredible!"

Thelma was still trying to take stock of her location. It felt like she had been gone for hours, but it was still relatively dark out. The sun was just starting to lighten the sky. She reached into her pocket for the dust she had collected, but there was nothing there. The only thing that had transported was her.

"What was it like in there, Thelma? Did you see your dad?" Alexander asked.

Thelma got up and dusted herself off. She walked toward the table and sat down, dropping her head into her hands to quell the dull ache she felt.

"No. She's keeping him in there—"

"Who? The ghost lady? You met her? Why didn't you give the necklace back?"

"Yes. I saw her. It's … she doesn't want the necklace. That place, it's terrible. So cold and dusty. And it makes your bones hurt, and you feel this … this hunger. But it's worse than hunger and doesn't go away."

She really wanted breakfast. Something warm. Waffles maybe, or eggs and toast. Maybe some hot cider. If the sun was almost up, then it was breakfast time.

"What did the ghost say?" Izzy demanded, barely able to contain her eagerness.

"Her name is Annabelle, and she's not … evil … I guess." Thelma wanted to tell them everything. All the stuff Annabelle had said about the women in their family and the "light" and how it kind of made her think of the weird glowing at Magistrate's Manse. But it was all tangled up in a confusing feeling of secrecy. She'd keep it to herself until she had a better understanding of what was going on.

"What?" Alexander was completely perplexed.

Thelma spied the box. She didn't know how exactly, but she had a job to do. She had to find Zachariah Understone's house and return it. She had to do it for her father and for Annabelle. Understone had put a curse on her family two hundred years ago, and Thelma was going to break it.

"We have work to do."

Two hours later, Izzy dashed through the front door with her arms full of research material. Between the three of them, Thelma, Izzy, and Alexander had managed to slide the bookcase just enough to get the door open so they didn't need to clamber through the window. Alexander was sitting in the middle of the living room floor with Henry Bee's laptop open in front of him on one side and a notebook on the other. Thelma had the cursed jewelry box carefully turned on its side and was munching on her third piece of buttered raisin toast.

"Um … *Dis, ek* um … *gayeta*, I guess?" She tried to sound out the strange words that were carved into the bottom of the box in between bites.

"Thelma, just read me the letters, OK? Can you take a break from chewing long enough to do that?" Typically, Thelma would be annoyed at such a request, but Alexander's intensity indicated that he was onto something. He was trying to transcribe the inscription so he could look the meaning up on the Internet. It was a language none of them had seen before.

"Fine," she said, "OK, there's like an *a* with a thing over it?" She twisted her mouth in a confused expression.

"Just let me see the box," Alexander said, looking over her shoulder and squinting. *"Dís, ek gæta þín í myrkri. Ek mun koma til þín hverjum hundraði árum ok spyrja, 'vildu mik eiga—*OK, I got it."

Izzy plopped her material down on the couch. "OK," she said. "I've got road maps, terrain maps, bus schedules, and hiking trail guides. I had to tell the librarian that I was working on a geography project. I was waiting for her like a creep outside the library at opening time so she thinks I'm completely insane. Also, here."

She dropped a large old tome on the floor next to Alexander. It was the town history of Marlomet.

Alexander examined the cover. "This might be very, very useful." Thelma picked it up and flipped through a few pages.

"Looks like mostly records. Births. Deaths. That kind of stuff."

"Property records?" he asked.

Thelma checked the index. "Bingo!"

Thelma, Alexander, and Izzy were all deep into their investigation when Eugene knocked on the door. He walked in with Ricky and Menkin, whose look of nervousness from last night had not disappeared.

"Can somebody fill me in on what's going on here? I have the feeling we definitely missed something," Eugene said as he surveyed the scene.

Thelma put down the Marlomet book and placed one hand on her hip. She turned to them matter-of-factly.

"Eugene," she began. "I'm going to tell you something that might make you mad. But instead of getting mad, you have to help us, OK?"

Eugene rolled his eyes and dropped his head. "I guess the correct response is 'yes, ma'am'?"

"I used the key and got sucked into the box."

"What!?" Menkin, Ricky, and Eugene gasped in almost perfect unison.

Izzy piped up, exasperated. "As you can see, she's totally fine. But we've got work to do."

"It's true," Thelma said, nodding. "Here's the deal. A long time ago my great-great-great-great," she paused trying to remember how many greats she needed, "great-great aunt was cursed by a bad guy who's probably also some kind of dark wizard. She's stuck in there, and she basically kidnapped my dad to get our

attention. Now we have to take the box and return it to the wizard guy. His name is Zachariah Understone, and we're figuring out where his house used to be so we can take this thing there and leave it. Hopefully that will break the spell, and my dad and Annabelle will be free."

The three adults stood, silent and dumbstruck.

"Oh, yeah, the ghost's name is Annabelle. She's kind of nice. Terrifying still, but kind of nice. Most of the time. Despite, you know, questionable ... methods. Anyway, Understone's property is probably about an hour's drive away, so that's where you guys come in."

Ricky ran his pudgy fingers through his hair. "I haven't even had coffee yet."

"It's Old Norse!" Alexander exclaimed from his position on the floor.

"The inscription?" Thelma asked as she rushed to his side to look at the screen.

"Yeah, look here."

Alexander had typed the words from the chest into an automatic translator, and after the annoying spinning of the little digital wheel stopped, these words popped up in the translation box:

Disiri, kept in darkness. Once every hundred years I shall visit you and ask once again that you be mine.

Thelma felt a twisting in her stomach.

"What's *Disiri* mean?" asked Menkin.

"Wait a second," Izzy said, putting the timeline

together in her head. She leaned over the computer. "Does that mean ..."

"He's going to visit her tonight. Tonight is the one time in a hundred years. That's why it was so important to Annabelle ..." Thelma's voice trailed off.

Alexander squinted and read it again. "There must be some kind of a portal that opens up into her world so he can reach her. If we return the gift to his property and he opens up the portal, maybe that creates the opportunity for her to break free."

Little by little, it was starting to make a strange kind of sense. And Thelma was getting the idea that this might not be a simple task. Annabelle said there would be danger, and there had been some secret in her eyes. What would happen if Understone emerged? Thelma's mind raced through a hundred different scenarios. Menkin had a good question: What was a Disiri? Annabelle wouldn't send Thelma into a trap, would she?

Eugene exchanged a nervous glance with Ricky and then turned to Thelma.

"When do we leave?"

"Tonight," she said.

Alexander spent the rest of the day turning Thelma's living room into a research library. He buried himself in books and documentation, studying area maps, local family lineage, Old Norse, even immigration records from the 1800s.

Around lunchtime, Thelma set down a sloppy peanut butter and jelly sandwich for him with a glass of ginger ale and a bowl of popcorn. Alexander looked up foggily.

"1816—that's the year Annabelle was taken," he said. "You know what's weird about 1816?"

Thelma could think of a lot of things, freshest in her mind was that it seemed pretty normal for teenagers to get married. She shook her head to banish the yuck.

"It was the year without a summer," Alexander continued. "It actually snowed in June! Can you imagine? And there were reportedly visible spots on the sun. The average person could view them without a telescope! I mean, can you imagine?"

"That is super weird." Thelma grabbed her notebook. She wrote down "1816—no summer" on a fresh page. No time now, but this was definitely a weather anomaly worthy of investigation.

Alexander smiled and laughed quietly before returning to his work. She wasn't sure what he was looking for in those books exactly, but she knew enough about him to trust his process.

She decided to prepare for the evening's mission in a different way. Thelma walked outside into the fresh air and breathed deep. She grabbed her pen and notebook out of her pocket and walked toward the river.

The earthy smell settled her mind a little. It was

familiar and good and muddy. The river made her feel steady—a funny thing since it never ever stopped moving.

Thelma plopped down on a patch of dry grass and opened her notebook. The pages were scrawled with notes from the past few days, observations on the supernatural.

Can be invisible

Can be visible

Can speak so quietly that a recorder picks up the sound but no one else hears it

Can speak so loud that you have to cover your ears

She grimaced, reading the list over—contradiction after contradiction. She searched for patterns in the evidence but it just made her dizzy and frustrated.

Thelma groaned and lay back, reclining on the soft, cool ground. The bright golden trees danced in the breeze. A woodpecker knocked in the distance. A sparrow flew across her frame of vision. She closed her eyes. She was so tired and heavy feeling that the earth felt like a welcoming mattress beneath her body. When sleep crept over her, she didn't fight it.

Her dream was indistinct and confusing, but not unhappy. Something about the sky and bird kingdoms and old books. Then, in perfect dream logic, there appeared the bear from the Riverfish third-grade pageant. It wasn't two kids in a bear suit, though, it was a real brown bear. She noticed that he was accompanied by a gigantic deer with large black eyes. The deer was trying to tell her something important, but just kept making a tsking sound. "Tsk, tsk, tsk …"

Thelma opened her eyes groggily to the inquisitive stare of a gray squirrel, greedily working on a nut, "tsk, tsk, tsk."

"Hey," she said. The squirrel bolted off up a nearby cedar tree, obviously suspicious that Thelma was after its lunch.

Thelma checked her watch. It had been a short nap, only a half hour, but she felt revived. As she yawned and stretched, she looked around the yard and a little blossom of guilt took root in her belly—she'd totally abandoned the orchid project since all of the trouble with her dad happened. She rubbed her eyes and walked over to the experimental orchid. Thelma's eyes widened and jaw dropped. Green sprouts curved out of the soil—definitely longer than they were before. The orchid was growing.

She ran into the shed and searched for something to root in the ground next to the orchid for support. The vanilla orchid was a vining plant and would need something to climb—she hadn't actually been prepared for this so soon. Thelma scanned the cramped shed for anything usable. Finally, she spotted a portion of a garden trellis that had broken apart during tropical storm Norma last summer. All that remained was about three feet of wood lattice. She grabbed it ran back out to the orchid.

How did this happen so quickly? Thelma's heart skipped and jumped in her chest. She bent down to touch the green shoots and as she did, warmth spread through her whole body. An image appeared to her then with such clarity that it shocked her a little. A fully blooming orchid—slender petaled, beautiful, and proud. Thelma smiled. She secured the piece of trellis and leaned it up against a nearby tree. Then she grabbed her notebook and sketched exactly what she'd seen in her mind's eye. The flower would grow. She knew it in her gut.

Day 6: Experimental specimen—green vines growing. Four inches in length. Provided stability for continued growth.

When she ran inside and told Alexander, he laughed out loud and clapped. "Amazing," he said, shaking his head. "Impossible, and amazing."

The Road to the Marshes

Darkness imbued the sky as the entire Riverfish Valley Paranormal Society, along with Alexander and Thelma, took to the road in Gary Indiana.

"This makes perfect sense," Thelma said as she looked over Izzy's shoulder. Izzy was studying a map of Marlomet. There was a deliberate red *x* on the location they believed to be Understone's property. "Annabelle said that he lived by a marsh. I'd bet anything that this is the right place."

"All the data match up." Alexander wiped his glasses with the bottom of his T-shirt in the crowded back seat. Menkin had expressed reservations about participating, but decided at the last minute that she would come along, much to Izzy's outspoken disappointment. Not only was she going to freak out, Izzy had argued, "but you're only supposed to have three people in the back seat." They had four people as well as an old cursed jewelry box, which sat on Thelma's lap inside her red backpack. Ricky munched on a handful of caramel popcorn in the front seat, and Eugene concentrated on the road.

"So, Ricky," Menkin began, her timid voice sounding shaky. "What is the plan if this man … er, wizard person is actually there?"

"Well, if he's there, he won't be in corporeal form," Alexander began.

"Corporeal?'" Menkin asked.

"Yeah, um, he won't have a body. Probably. He'll probably be a ghost. I highly doubt we're going to come across a 230-year-old man tonight."

"Right," she said, clearly not comforted, "So, the term *Disiri?*"

"Don't worry about it, Menkin. I'll take care of us." Ricky turned back and gave her a reassuring smile. He had a popcorn kernel stuck between his two front teeth. Menkin didn't seem to notice. She just smiled and said, "You always do," in her sweet but nasally voice.

"Know where I always feel safe?" Izzy quipped. "At a gas station. Oh look! There's one right now! Let's drop Menkin off. So she's safe." She shot Menkin an exasperated and spiteful look.

They had passed the Marlomet town center about twenty-five minutes earlier. Marlomet was a pretty fun town. No Applekin Festivals or anything, but it had a famous ice cream shop, Chilly Willy's. Thelma closed her eyes and wished that she were out for a drive with Mom and Dad after dinner.

Mom, Dad, and Thelma Bee venture out to Chilly Willy's for a treat. Thelma orders her favorite, chocolate-chocolate-chocolate chip on a waffle cone, and her dad opts for a home-made Italian ice, cherry-flavored. Mom gets a strawberry shake. For the whole ride home, they blast the radio and make up their own words to popular songs. When they reach their warm, comfy home, all three Bees settle in together to watch an old Audrey Hepburn movie, or that documentary on dinosaurs Dad's been talking about for a month.

"Will you two be quiet for a minute?" Eugene said, interrupting a spat between Ricky and Izzy, as well as Thelma's daydream. "I'm trying to concentrate. The GPS is going crazy. I don't think it knows where we are." Thelma must have zoned out for a while, because they were far away from Marlomet now.

And Eugene was right about the GPS. The virtual map blinked and changed over and over again. And there were no more streetlights on the road. Maybe that meant they were getting close.

Gary Indiana headed down the road at a good clip when suddenly something huge and dark darted out onto the street. Eugene slammed on the brakes. Ricky yelled, "Watch out!!"

Everyone screamed as seatbelts tightened. The car swerved violently to avoid the animal, but they collided with a deafening crash. Thelma's head hit the back of the seat hard before the car stopped moving. Her head pounded so hard she could hear it in her ears. The box in the backpack had dug into her during the collision and her arms and torso felt sore and bruised. Eugene unbuckled his seatbelt and turned frantically around to the backseat.

"Is everyone OK?"

Just as Thelma was about to respond, the car moved again, but it was not Eugene driving—and they were not moving forward. There was a hard impact on the side of the car, and Eugene was thrown over Ricky's lap. That same huge, very strong animal pushed the car sideways, toward the edge of the road. It didn't make sense, but the beast seemed determined to destroy Gary Indiana. One huge jolt flung the unseatbelted Eugene even farther, and his head hit the passenger door with a cracking sound.

"Eugene!" cried Thelma,

"Ricky, is he OK?" She tried to get a look and thought she saw blood.

Ricky looked around wildly and tried to apply pressure to Eugene's forehead with his arm, "He passed out," said Ricky, then the car moved again, "Oh crud, no! Everyone just hang on!"

The car moved with increasing speed. Thelma looked out of the window but could see nothing but black. Not the black of night, but the black fur of the animal that was aggressively pushing Gary Indiana into a roadside ditch.

"What is that?" Izzy shrieked.

"I don't know!" Thelma answered. She was terrified.

"It's a …" Alexander's eyes were as big as flying saucers. "It's a bull!" he yelled. The words escaped him just as the car flipped.

The next moments were a complete blur. She remembered Eugene hitting the ceiling and guarding her face against the airborne backpack. There were crushing sounds and screaming sounds and the feeling of being totally out of control. Thelma's brain turned to a station that only broadcast static and she closed her eyes tight. She opened them just in time to see Eugene's toolbox, which had been near her feet, become airborne and nearly crash into her head. Except that it stopped an inch away from her face in seeming defiance of gravitational laws. It was impossible.

The car suddenly stopped with a hard impact

against a tree—they were back on four tires. For a moment, everything was very quiet. No one else had seen the toolbox—just Thelma. She felt like she should tell someone what happened, but felt lost for words. Again, she felt that now-familiar uncomfortable secrecy.

Eventually, Thelma heard a quiet whimpering coming from Izzy. She looked around. Menkin and Alexander were alert, and Ricky was breathing heavily, holding Eugene's face in his hands.

"He's OK," he finally said. "He's breathing. Let's get out of here."

Thelma unbuckled her seatbelt and grabbed her backpack. The car was right-side up again, but it was pretty clear that Gary Indiana had seen his last road trip. The side door was utterly crushed, and there was smoke pouring out of the crumpled hood.

"We've got to move away from the car," Menkin said. "Up the hill. Come on." She took one side of Eugene and Ricky took the other. They dragged him up the hill to a relatively clear spot under an oak tree, which would have probably looked fiery red in the daylight. They propped Eugene up against the trunk, and everyone sat down to catch their breath. Thelma grabbed at the cool grass nervously.

Izzy was quiet and pale. She trembled and looked around. "What—what could have done that?" she asked in a whisper.

Alexander was also shaken. His glasses had broken in half, and he grasped the frames in his hand. "It was a wild bull. I swear!" His eyes were wide with confusion and fear. "I know it doesn't make any sense. It was far … far too big and … rabid, apparently. It must have been rabid. Geez, do bulls get rabies? They must, right? I really don't know how to quantify …"

His brow furrowed; he continued, "Yeah. It's impossible. But I know what I saw. And it was huge. Just huge."

Izzy wiped her face and shook her head. Her usual bravery seemed to have slipped away. Thelma thought about Izzy's parents and their car accident. She reached out and put a comforting hand on Izzy's shoulder and she could feel her friend's frame quake.

Izzy clasped Thelma's hand.

Ricky was tending to Eugene by the tree when Eugene let out series of painful-sounding coughs. He opened his eyes.

"Gary Indiana?" Eugene asked weakly.

Ricky just shook his head, indicating the sad fate of Eugene's longtime road companion. Eugene grimaced.

Menkin stood on the side of the road. She was checking her cell phone for reception. It was quiet. No cars came or went. She marched back down to the group, a serious look on her face.

"OK, we've got no cell reception here. So this is what's going to happen. Ricky, you stay here with Eugene and these guys. I'm going to walk to that gas station we passed. That was probably about five miles back, I'd guess. Just stay here, OK? So I can find you again. I'll come back with help." Everyone nodded, and she started to walk off. Then she paused and turned around. "Don't go near the car. It could blow." She left.

"She really shines in emergency situations," Alexander said.

Ricky nodded with a shy smile. "Yeah—she can be pretty amazing."

Izzy, even in her delicate state, managed a stadium-sized eye roll.

Thelma was deep in thought. There were no wild humungous bulls around here. That was insane. But she believed Alexander—she had no reason to doubt him. She had a chilling realization.

"It was him," Thelma said as she walked back over to the group.

"What?" Ricky asked.

"Understone. It had to be him. He's trying to keep us away from his property. He doesn't want Annabelle freed. He doesn't want us meddling in his business."

"I don't know if we should jump to that conclusion." Ricky said, putting his hands up in a plaintive gesture. He obviously didn't like where this was going.

"No," Izzy interjected, dusting herself off. "Thelma's right. It makes perfect sense. He uses dark magic, right?"

"And it's utterly improbable that a wild bull would head-butt a car and push it down a hill and into a ditch. It doesn't make any sense. Also, where did it go?" Alexander rose from his seated position and squinted as he tried to survey the area without his glasses.

He was right. There weren't even any visible tracks.

Izzy was starting to sound more like her usual spunky self. "Of course! He conjured up the bull to try to stop us!"

Ricky raised his voice. "Listen! Just—just calm down, OK? So, what if you're right? What then? If that's really Understone, then he isn't just some spirit. He's dangerous. Like, real-life dangerous. Look what he's done!" He gestured toward Eugene, who was still groggy and sitting against the tree trunk.

"He's right," Thelma said, a surge of excitement rising up inside of her.

"Thank you." Ricky exhaled.

"It's way too dangerous for you guys. I'm going on alone." She said this because she meant it. Something was going on and it had to do with her. With her and her family. Thelma swung the backpack around her shoulders and pointed forward.

"What? No!" Ricky shouted. "No one is going anywhere! Didn't you hear Menkin? She's going to come back with help, so we have to stay put. Everyone."

Thelma started walking, feeling a little guilty for defying him, but completely determined to go on.

"Thelma, you're not going anywhere—do you hear me?" Ricky yelled with a nervous voice, one that was unused to being raised.

"Or what, Ricky?" she snapped back, "Are you going to tell my dad? My mom?" The force of her own voice startled Thelma. Ricky stood silent, frustrated.

At that moment, she truly believed what she had been saying all along. There was no choice, no other path.

Ricky sighed and put his head in his hands. "I can't leave Eugene," he said, defeated.

"I know," Thelma said. She tried to comfort Ricky. "I'll be safe." She turned toward the road. She was surprised to see both Alexander and Izzy standing there, waiting for her.

"I calculated the probability of us letting you do this alone," he said.

"Zero," Izzy added.

"Guys ..." Thelma knew she should fight for them to stay behind, but her desperate need for their companionship won out.

"Izzy! Isabel Finkle!!!" Ricky's voice got fainter and fainter as the three friends walked farther down the deserted autumn road.

"I kind of feel bad," Alexander said.

"For Ricky?" Izzy snipped. "No way. He's fine. He's probably just scared that his girlfriend will be mad if we're not there when she gets back."

"Girlfriend? Really?" Thelma asked. "Menkin?"

"I don't know—that's my guess, though. He thinks he can pull one over on me, but I have eyes. I see the dumb looks they give each other," Izzy said.

"Is that why you're so mean to her all the time?" Alexander asked.

"Oh come on! She's a big scaredy-cat! She's super lame. And ... and her name is dumb ..."

"Seems nice enough to me," Thelma said.

"And pretty handy in a life-threatening situation," Alexander added.

"Great. Well, why don't you ask her to be your girl-friend?" Izzy smirked.

Alexander became quiet and also slightly maroon at the suggestion. "Highly unlikely," he muttered.

"Quiet!" Izzy issued a loud whisper and froze.

"What is it?" Thelma asked.

"I heard something. In the trees," she said.

Thelma stopped moving and peered into the forest that seemed to be encroaching around them. It was dark, and the narrowing road had very few lights. The full moon above illuminated the treetops. There was barely a breeze to ruffle the leaves.

Suddenly a wind seemed to emerge from inside the trees themselves. Thelma, followed by Izzy and Alexander, ran off the road and hid behind a large rock. A loud wave of flapping began and intensified until it propelled a murder of crows up through the forest and above the treetops, eclipsing the moon entirely.

"Dumb birds," said Izzy, after the flapping subsided. Everyone's adrenaline was pumping. Apparently even a flock of birds had the potential to send them into a panic.

They were only a short way down the road when they came to an intersection. A dirt path veered off to the right, unmarked and muddy.

"I don't think Gary Indiana would have had much luck here anyway," said Alexander.

"This is our turn." Thelma pointed after consulting

the hand-drawn map in her pocket. "This is Puffer's Path."

"Are you sure?" said Alexander. "It's not marked."

"It's official enough for us." Thelma patted him on the back, and they began their trip down Puffer's Path. Thelma led the pack, extending her hands out in front of her to feel the way when she could no longer see. Thin branches hit her palms and her shoulders as she trudged through. She hadn't wanted to put Izzy or Alexander in danger, but Thelma was grateful for the company now. This place was creepy. The moon was full and bright but sometimes obscured by the tall trees overhead. They were moving at a slow clip, tripping over raised roots and stepping directly into muddy puddles, which soaked their sneakers.

"Gross." Thelma grunted as her foot squished. The mosquitoes were getting more aggressive too, even though the night was cool.

"Ow!" Izzy slapped her own face, trying to catch a biting bug. "This probably means we're near water," she added, rubbing her cheek for comfort.

"Yes, exactly," Thelma said. She pulled out her map once more and pointed. "We're going to come up to the Soapybone River real soon. That runs all the way into the Marlomet marshes. That's where we're headed."

"I hope we get there soon," Alexander said.

A screeching, awful sound rose from the darkness of the forest. It was something Thelma had never heard before. It sounded like a human screaming, but slightly different—more feral, wild, and loud.

Izzy and Thelma rushed together with high-pitched shrieks, sandwiching Alexander.

"What was that?" Izzy whispered hoarsely, her eyes darting around the dark forest.

"It wasn't a bull, that's for sure," Thelma said.

"Ladies," Alexander said. "Everyone just calm down, OK?"

He relished this moment of superiority.

"Fisher cat," said Alexander in that know-it-all tone that drove Thelma bananas.

"A what?" Thelma asked.

"A fisher cat. They mostly eat birds, mice, small mammals, cats …"

"Ew!" Izzy made a face.

"Yes," he continued. "But we're not cats, so there's really no need to worry. It just has a particularly distinct sound."

"I'll say." Izzy detangled herself from the group. "Sounds like a nightmare.

Some kind of demon or something. It's about the worst thing I've ever heard."

"Hey, Thelma," Alexander said. "Izzy's never heard you sing?" He was having a good laugh for himself until Thelma shoved him and he fell backward with a splash, directly into a mud puddle.

"You're hilarious," she snorted, walking down the path.

Izzy was right about being close to water. Within minutes they heard the rushing sound of the river. Thelma could also smell it. It was a familiar scent, heavy and earthy like in her backyard at home. Thelma grabbed onto a leafy branch in front of her and pushed it aside so that she could see—there it was, the Soapybone River.

Mom had told Thelma that early settlers named the river because the rushing rapids created a soap-like froth as it crashed up against, or twisted around, the huge pale rocks that peeked up out of the water. However it got its name, it definitely looked like a body of water you would not want to jump in. Unless, of course, you had a raft, guide, and helmet.

Thelma's imagination drifted momentarily to her family's Grand Canyon trip last summer—right before she started middle school. She wanted to be there again. Weird, she thought, how you never appreciate things enough when they're happening, in the moment. Not just the super cool stuff like Grand Canyon trips either. Boring stuff like going boot shopping with Mom or helping Dad categorize the shop's silverware.

She'd give anything to time travel back to the shop now, just polishing spoons and putting them in little piles. Thelma made a quiet promise that if they ever escaped all of this, if she was ever together and safe with her mom and dad again, she would really appreciate it 100 percent.

"Thelma!" Izzy hollered. "The path is getting too muddy!"

"Yeah," Alexander added. "It's just about disappeared."

It was true. Puffer's Path was overwhelmed with bushes, vines, and roots to the point where it actually wasn't much of a path at all anymore. Thelma peeked her head around the brush.

"We might be able to follow the river by walking along the outside of the tree line here." As she peered over, Thelma saw that it was about a three-foot drop from where they'd be walking to the water. And the small ledge of solid ground was pretty narrow.

"We just have to hold onto the trees," Izzy added

as she walked up next to Thelma and took a look. "It's doable."

Alexander joined the two girls tentatively. The moonlight looked beautiful on the river and even made some of the jutting stones sparkle a little bit.

He sighed. "OK. It's not like we can turn around and go back, right?"

"Not unless you want to get eaten by a fisher cat," Thelma said.

"Or get kidnapped by a weirdo, or gored and killed by a homicidal bull," Izzy added.

She then secured her yellow braid and grabbed the narrow trunk of a white-barked tree. She swung effortlessly around and planted both feet on the narrow ledge of earth between the tree line and the three-foot slope that gave way to the Soapybone River. Thelma glanced back at Alexander, then followed suit.

"Good perspective," Alexander said. He grabbed the sturdiest looking tree branch in sight and scuffed his feet awkwardly behind the two girls.

River Creature Facts

(OBSERVED)

Thelma scooted one foot after the next along the ledge of dirt. Her hands felt like they were being slowly ripped apart by the trees' bark and branches that she clung to, and her backpack started to strain her shoulders. "How are you guys doing?" she yelled to Alexander and Izzy.

Izzy was finding this all very easy, it seemed. She was extremely small and had the agility of a professional gymnast. "Piece of cake!" she yelled back.

"I—I'm fine, Thelma. No worries here," Alexander's voice cracked, a dead giveaway that he was in rough shape.

Thelma tried to concentrate on other things besides the increasingly painful blisters she was getting on the palms of her hands. Thelma thought of Understone's property. Was there still a house there? That seemed unlikely. Annabelle said this was the two hundredth anniversary—plenty of time for new construction to take over.

Then her thoughts turned to the bull. Was it really some kind of manifestation of Understone's magic? It was the size of a small house, after all. And the way it attacked Eugene's car seemed so deliberate.

Thelma was shaken from her thoughts by a deep, gurgling that was so loud she almost let go of the trees to cover her ears.

"What was that, Alexander?" she yelled. He was about eight feet behind her at this point. "Some kind of harmless river … tree thing or something?"

She hoped to hear his know-it-all voice tell her something reassuring. Instead, she heard nothing. Alexander had frozen and was clutching the trees.

"Alexander?"

"I have no idea what that was!" he yelled back.

Thelma felt the ground beneath her feet rumble slightly, the way a room shakes a little when someone's playing the radio too loud. The moon illuminated the river, and all went quiet.

"I think it's gone, whatever it wa—"

Before she could even finish her sentence, Izzy's tiny body was swept from the ledge and into the air by a massive claw, white and slick.

"Izzy!" Alexander screamed at the top of his lungs, letting go of the branches and nearly tumbling into the water.

"Alexander, get into the trees!" Thelma yelled

as she tried to swing around and squeeze her body between two tree trunks.

What she saw then defied reason. The creature that emerged was nearly as wide as the river itself. Its white bumpy head turned smooth around its small yellow eyes, like they were lost in a mass of slimy flesh. The head was a troll-like lump coming out of a wide and scaly pair of white shoulders. One of the creature's white, slimy claws held onto a large river rock. The other was clasped around Izzy's waist.

Thelma's mom often told stories of strange, dangerous creatures in the wild, but never anything quite like this. Thelma was terrified and transfixed. In its fist, Izzy kicked and screamed like she was on fire.

The creature turned from side to side, as if it was searching. Thelma had to do something. Her muscles felt frozen, but she gritted her teeth and forced herself to action. She felt around the ground and found a rock so large she could just barely palm it. Holding onto a tree with one hand, she threw the rock at the creature with all her strength. It landed like a pebble against the monster's pale skin.

It swung its massive frame around to face Thelma directly. That's when she saw it. On the side of the lumpish head there was a large dark purple scar in a shape of a bull's head, two horns pointing up toward the creature's snarling mouth. Thelma shrieked involuntarily. Suddenly it was so clear. Hilda Hillbrook's birthmark, the bull, the monster's scar—it was all tied together. One dark force: Understone.

"Let her go!" Thelma screamed, hurling another rock, and then trying to steady herself.

The monster lumbered up to where Thelma was hanging on and looked at her. It didn't strike her or try to swipe her off of the ledge she balanced on, but it glared directly at her.

She broke out in a cold sweat and tried to summon the bravery to reach for another rock since she had the monster's face at such close proximity. Izzy, taking advantage of the moment, moved her body like an electrified wire in the monster's hold. With one powerful kick, she hit the creature in the face with her big black boot. For a moment it loosened his grasp, and she wriggled out through its fingers.

The monster let out an angry hiss and turned its attention back to its escaping prey. With incredible skill and balance, Izzy ran over the width of the thing's disgusting shoulders and made a flying leap to the other side of the river. The monster grabbed her by the leg mid-leap but couldn't keep hold of her. Izzy fell into the river with a splash, and Thelma once again heard the monster's long, low hiss.

In the river, Izzy looked like she was as expert a swimmer as she was a climber. She moved deftly through the cold water.

"Go! Go! I'm OK!" Izzy screamed as her head popped up out of the water. It rushed fast, carrying her downstream. The monster rose up momentarily, revealing a crusted and tentacled belly before soundlessly descending back into the water and out of sight.

"Izzy!" Alexander looked to the river in desperation. His voice cracked as he screamed. "Izzy!!!" There was no answer.

Energy Demanding Transport

(PUSHING THROUGH)

Thelma and Alexander sat terrified and huddled together at the foot of an old oak tree in the middle of the longest night of their lives.

"She'll be fine," Thelma quietly repeated to herself a few times, holding her knees to her chest. Her clothes were wet, and dead leaves clung to her everywhere.

"What?" Alexander looked at her disbelieving. "What is fine about this? That thing was not … that thing was not real."

"Yes it was," said Thelma.

"And the water's so cold." Alexander stared at the ground, "I mean, in the very best case scenario she could still get hypothermia!"

"But she's Izzy," Thelma said, wanting to cry

but forcing a confident tone. "Right? I mean, did you see her kick that thing in the face?"

Alexander looked up. "Yeah."

They both fell silent, but they were thinking the same thing. What was that creature?

"It's Understone," Alexander said resolutely, which was exactly what Thelma had just been thinking.

"It is. I know it is," she agreed, "The bull, everything. It's him. He's trying to stop us from making it to his property and freeing Annabelle. But ..."

"What?" Alexander asked.

"Something about it's not right. Alexander, that monster didn't want me." Thelma tried to wipe the mud from her face. "It looked right at me, and it didn't try to knock me down or take me. It just looked at me."

"What do you think that means?" he asked.

"I don't know. But, it doesn't seem right." She paused. "There's something else."

"What?"

"In the car, when we were crashing, Eugene's toolbox was headed right for my face. But it just stopped. Like, mid-air," she dropped her head into her hands, "It doesn't make sense!"

"None of this does. It's starting to feel like some kind of trap." Alexander said quietly. "I mean, first Eugene gets hurt and now Izzy. I'm scared," He said.

"Me too," said Thelma.

"Really?"

"Yeah, are you kidding?" she asked.

"You just ... you never seem scared."

"Alexander, my dad is missing, and our friend was just attacked by some kind of river monster. We were in a car accident, and I'm only half sure of where we're going. I'm terrified," she said.

"That kind of makes me feel better," he said.

Thelma stared at her friend, confused. "You're the brave one, Alexander. Not me."

He scoffed, and stood to dust of his clothes.

"I'm being serious. You're scared but you're helping me anyway. You're trying to save *my* family." She wiped mud from her friend's shoulder, "That's, like, the definition of brave"

Alexander took a deep breath, wiped his face, and straightened up. "Let me take a look at the map," he said.

Thelma fumbled through her pocket and found the paper, now soggy with river water. "Not much good it's going to do us," she said.

Alexander looked around, squinting for lack of usable spectacles. "Well, we know we have to follow the river downstream, because that's where we'll find the marsh. And … wait here." He walked a few paces away from Thelma; she could hear leaves crunching under his feet.

"Over here!" he yelled. "Look—there's a trail, and it's going in the right direction. This way we won't have to climb around the river the rest of the way."

Thelma was relieved to find the path and move along, but she had a heavy feeling, like they were leaving Izzy behind. Eugene and Izzy were trying to help her, and they'd gotten hurt—who knows how badly. Thelma just wished that she'd been the one to get thrown around in the car and attacked by the river monster. But then who would save her dad?

Thelma knew one thing for certain. She was not going to let anything bad happen to Alexander.

After walking down the trail for just a few minutes, they emerged into a clearing. Tall trees gave way to lower brush and wetter ground—the Marlomet Marshes. They could see an open sky and constellations. Thelma was so familiar with the celestial patterns that they relaxed her a bit, burning bright and clear. Right away she spotted Orion's belt directly above them. One, two, three points of light in a row. It made her feel safe somehow. She breathed in deeply through her nose and out through her mouth.

The river lost its rushing current as it flowed into the marsh, like a piece of broccoli stuck in a milk straw. The water oozed around and puddled up unpredictably. Thelma had wished for good waterproof boots earlier in the evening, but the need was acute now. She tried her best not to think of all the slimy and squirmy things that might be slithering around her footfalls as they trekked along the edge of the marsh. In the distance they spied a dim light.

"Is that it?" asked Alexander.

"I think so. I mean, it's got to be, right?"

"Yeah." Alexander exhaled and bit his lip nervously.

"You don't have to come with me. I mean it," said Thelma.

Alexander shook his head to dismiss the notion and took a few deliberate, squishy steps forward. He motioned for her to follow. As they got closer, they saw that the light was coming from a house. It was not a large house, more like a cottage.

"This is the spot," Alexander whispered, "It wasn't on the most current map, of course, but it is pretty isolated out here. And there are plenty of houses in town that date back even further than the 1800s."

Thelma nodded and took a few slow, slopping steps toward the cottage. She mentally prepared a plan. She would just knock on the door and explain to the current owner of the cottage that it was possible his or her house was the location of some kind of inter-dimensional portal. Maybe it would be no big deal. Maybe the nice owner would offer them some tea with milk and sugar. Positive thinking.

She stopped abruptly, taken by a notion. She looked down at herself—her clothing, her shoes, the cuts on her hands, and the mud in her hair.

"I can't go in like this. I look like a crazy swamp person." She turned to Alexander.

"Thelma, seriously?" Alexander threw his head back in frustration.

"What? If someone who looked like I do right now knocked on my door at home, I'd call the police!"

"You have got to be kidding me!" Alexander looked as if he didn't know whether to laugh or be completely furious. "After everything we've been through these past few days … all the rules you've broken …

the life-threatening danger … you're going to stop now? Because your sneakers are dirty?"

"I'm a mess," she said.

Alexander laughed in exasperation and nodded, "I look good enough for the both of us," he said.

Thelma rolled her eyes and even laughed a little, giving up any notion of normalcy.

"OK." Alexander straightened up, "Let's go."

Incendiary Materials

(OBSERVED)

Thelma walked up to the door, adrenaline pumping through her body. She knocked tentatively and waited. No answer. She knocked again. Waited. Nothing. Someone had to be home, Thelma thought, because a light flickered inside.

The cottage was totally dilapidated looking. It was a miracle it was even standing, she thought. It was obvious that no one was taking great care to preserve this place.

"What do we do?" asked Alexander.

Thelma put her hand on the door. Wincing a little, she pushed.

It swung wide open. Both Thelma and Alexander jumped back in surprise.

"Hello?" Thelma called inside the cottage. "Hello, is anyone here?"

Silence.

The room inside was bare with the exception of an empty fireplace and one small table in the middle of the room. It looked unnervingly familiar, but she didn't know why. The floors had large boards, each the width of a tree trunk. On the table was a single burning candle, the source of dim light.

"Hello?" Alexander's voice fell flat in the chilled air.

"I don't think anybody's home," Thelma said.

"I don't think anybody has been home in a long time." He scanned the old space. There were thick cobwebs in each corner.

"Well, someone lit a candle so—" Thelma froze as soon as the words left her mouth. She knew exactly where she had seen a table like that before. It was where she sat with Annabelle. And the candle—it was the same candle too.

"It's him. He's here," Thelma whispered, the words like ice on her tongue.

Suddenly the candle extinguished with a soft hiss, and the door slammed shut behind Thelma and Alexander. They both stood very still, trying not to breathe too loud. Any warmth in the October air was utterly absent. The sneaky noise of creaking floorboards came from another room. Alexander reached down and grasped Thelma's hand with all of his might and she squeezed it back.

Thelma's eyes were trained on the blackened doorway that led deeper into the house. She tried to make out shapes in the darkness, but her eyes played tricks on her, forcing her to squint and blink.

Finally, after what seemed like forever, a long, thin cane swung into view and hit the floor-boards with a sharp thwack. The man who emerged from the doorway had black hair neatly combed back into a ponytail, the kind that may have been stylish in some long-ago time. His face was strange and almost hand-some in a way, but something about his eyes threw his counte-nance out of balance. They were light, too light. As though they had no color at all. Alexander shivered visibly.

"Miss Bee," the man said in a smooth voice. When his lips parted to speak, they revealed straight, yellowed teeth.

Thelma inhaled sharply. This was Zachariah Understone.

Why did he know her name?

"I'm so glad you could make it," he continued. "I was beginning to worry." His clear eyes darted to Alex-ander. "Who is your friend?"

"Understone," she whispered, the word catching in her throat.

"Yes" he said, grinning. "I see my reputation precedes me. Very well. I shall ask again. Who is this young man?"

"It's none of your business," Thelma snapped, and reflexively shoved Alexander behind her.

"I must disagree. I thought she would have eliminated all of your traveling companions by this time. Negligence on my part, I'm afraid. I must be getting old." He smiled and cackled softly to himself. "That's a bit of humor, Miss Bee." He sighed, seemingly disappointed that she wasn't laughing.

She? Who was this "she"? The monster in the river was a lady? Thelma was repulsed and fascinated at the same time by the strange notion.

"Either way, this is my property. And your little friend is, unfortunately, not invited to this particular occasion. Goodbye, boy."

Thelma felt Alexander's hand leave hers as his body flew off the ground and his back hit the ceiling with the sound of violent exhalation. Understone pointed one gloved finger at Alexander, and as it moved, so did he. His body slid across the ceiling as though he was nothing but a flimsy puppet, with no will of his own. Alexander's face was drained of color, and his mouth opened in shock as Understone, with a flick of his wrist, opened the front door and forced the boy's body out into the cool night, slamming the door again after his ejection.

Speechless, Thelma turned toward the door. She

wanted to run. She wanted to see if Alexander was OK, to get out of here and away from this. But she grounded her feet to the floor in defiance of all her instincts

What was Understone? He looked like a man, but there was something twitching and animalistic behind his stare. She gathered herself together and faced him with determination.

"Release her," said Thelma.

"I'm sorry, of whom do you speak, dear?"

"Annabelle," Thelma fumbled to unzip her backpack and present the box. "I know you cursed her and forced her into this thing." She placed it on the table between them, willing her hands not to shake. "Now you're going to let her out."

Understone's face spread into a wide yellow smile.

"Yes! It is so kind of you to return my property, Miss Bee. A fortunate evening for both of us, I daresay. How very serendipitous for a lovely young Disiri like yourself you to bring her back to me."

His eyes focused on her neck and then flashed in excitement. Thelma's heart sank. This was all his plan.

And there was that word again, Disiri. Thelma had no idea what he was talking about, or what a Disiri was—but she most certainly was not there to deliver Annabelle directly to her tormenter. And if she did, how could she get her dad back then? She summoned her bravery.

"I said release her, Understone!"

He didn't seem to register her words at all. He moved around the room like smoke, barely making a sound aside from his cane's thwack.

"My father is in there too," she added, immediately unsure if revealing that information was a good idea.

Understone raised his eyebrows and placed one hand on the box. A red glow formed under the palm of his hand. The sound that followed was somewhere in between a long cough and a hiss. Tiny black particles materialized out of the red glow and formed a swarm over Understone's hand. The black dots traveled toward Thelma. She raised her arms in defense, but noticed that the dots soon glommed together. Little by little, the particles joined each other, and before very long at all, her father was standing before her.

"Dad!!" she screamed and grabbed both his arms just as he was about to collapse to the floor. He looked awful, his skin had taken on a gray pallor, and his body was brittle. Thelma was overwhelmed by her dad's weight as he fell, but she eased him to the floor with some effort.

He opened his eyes and looked up at his daughter's face.

"Thelma," he whispered, and then smiled weakly. She took his hand in hers and squeezed. He felt cold, but he still had blood pumping through his veins. Her father was alive.

"Thank you," she said.

The words weren't out of her mouth before a low grunt escaped from Henry Bee and he slid unnaturally across the floor to Understone's feet. This man had an infuriating habit of treating the people she loved like rag dolls and Thelma felt her fear turning to fury. Understone looked at Henry Bee and then at the box from which he had just emerged.

He sighed. "I should punish her. I know I should."

"What? What are you talking about?" Thelma cried. "Leave my dad alone!"

"I shouldn't be naive" he grinned coolly, "I knew she'd enlist the help of her little sister witch somehow, and I suppose this was her way."

Thelma bristled. Annabelle sent her here knowing the danger. Understone had expected her—it was as if she was the only one who wasn't in on the plan. Her belly burned with anger.

"You Disiri are so adorably arrogant," Understone continued. "She really thinks that you, a child, are strong enough to … what? Overpower me? Set her free? It's sweet, really. So like the Annabelle I knew. And, of course, I love her." He gestured dramatically, "Oh, and love will make you do wild, terrible things … won't it?" He looked at Thelma as though he actually expected her to commiserate. She began to realize that Zachariah Understone was even more of a maniac than she initially thought. Love? He really thought that he and Annabelle would live happily ever after? Even after holding her captive and stealing her from her life?

"Annabelle will never marry you. Just let her go."

Understone glared at Thelma, "You know nothing

of it, witch." He spit the word. "Do you understand, Miss Bee, what it means to have pride in one's work?"

"What?" Thelma was bewildered. He shifted moods so suddenly it was hard to follow. Her dad was still slumped on the floor across the room and Thelma was desperate to get him and get out of there.

"I ..." Understone pruned up his face, but then his expression lightened. He sighed thoughtfully but with some frustration, searching for the right words. He picked the wooden box up with both hands.

"I designed this with so much care, you see. It feels, very much, like an extension of myself. Sacred. A holy place for my most precious possession, do you understand? And Annabelle—dear, dear, fickle Annabelle desecrated my creation by inviting in this," he said, gesturing to Thelma's dad, half-conscious on the floor, "this thing!"

Thelma considered her options and thought of Annabelle, who was still stranded in the box, but then she looked at her father lying helplessly on the floor. She decided that enough was enough. Saving Annabelle was not as vital as getting her dad to safety. And the more she learned, the more it seemed like Annabelle knew exactly what kind of danger she'd sent Thelma into, which was not cool—even for an imprisoned ghost.

This Understone, this guy, thing, whatever he was, was truly dangerous. And Alexander was out there alone, and they had to find Izzy. They had to escape.

"Listen, Mr. Understone." Thelma tried to sound

respectful. Maybe if she just let him have the box, this could all be over. "I, um, me and my dad, we're just going to take off I think …"

Still lost in his reverie, Understone interrupted: "… But how could I punish my poor Annabelle? She is my love, and she has returned to me. And she has brought me such a gift. Such a wonderful gift." He turned his creepy, translucent gaze to Thelma. Her skin prickled.

"Um, I don't …"

"You are alive, little sister Disiri," he said in a near whisper, "and in my grasp."

"No. My name is Thelma. Thelma Bee," she said, flustered, "I'm eleven years old. I don't know who Disiri is, I'm sorry."

He laughed, exposing his long yellowed teeth. "You are so young, Miss Bee. Can it really be that you know nothing? Just as well. My girl. My dearest little thing, you have something that I need."

Dependent and Independent Variables

Understone reached one gloved hand out to Thelma's neck and she froze in fear.

"Your key, my dear." His form cast a long dark shadow on the wall in the moonlight, making him seem even taller than he was.

"I don't have my keys with me, they're probably crushed in Gary Indiana," she stammered.

Understone laughed with joyless eyes. He was getting impatient. "The stone you wear around your neck, little witch. That is your key, and you must give it to me. Now."

Something inside of Thelma rose up at that moment. It was instinct and not reason that answered Mr. Understone's request. Thelma looked him squarely in the eyes and said, "No."

He reached into his coat and pulled out a

small box. "A trade then." He opened it to reveal a large, expensive looking ruby ring. Thelma remembered Annabelle's story. This is the ring he used to "propose" to her—if you could call what was basically a mugging a marriage proposal.

"No! I will not marry you! I'm eleven and you're old and, like, not human I think, and …"

"Marry you?" the laughter that came from Understone sounded almost sincere. "What a foolish, preposterous girl you are. Firstly, I am not human as you've guessed with all of your powerful deductive abilities, second, I have only one love." His tone sobered and he put a gentle hand on the antique box. "One beautiful love, perfect in all ways besides one—her fickle heart. I will only be with my Annabelle, and she with me."

"She doesn't want you! You kept her prisoner!"

"Silence!" he sneered, losing his humor. "It's this terrible place, this terrible world that clouds her judgment. Once we are away, in a more civilized world, she will be mine, this I know. That is why I need your key, witch."

"I'm not a witch."

"You proud Disiris are all the same. Glorified hags and nothing more. It's your key that I need, and your key that I will take one way or another. I was offering you a trade, but that may have given you the wrong impression," he replied, an artificially saccharine tone in his voice, "You are going to give me the key. Or you will be very sorry that you did not. This evening ends with my reunion with my sweet bride, and our leaving this terrible earthly realm. This is accomplished by a living Disiri—you, dear girl—giving me a key—that necklace."

Understone grabbed Thelma's hand, bringing it up to his lips in a gesture designed to taunt. She had to fight a sudden surge in her stomach that wanted her to double over sick.

Then something out the window caught her eye. She couldn't be sure, but for just a split second she could have sworn that she saw the flash of a long blonde braid in the moonlight.

"Hey!" A tiny silhouette appeared under the half-opened window. Izzy, muddy from head to toe and furious, stood with one hand on her hip, the other clutching a long piece of rope.

Understone pivoted to see who was there, and as he turned, another body flew through the window and landed on top of him. They both fell to the floor with a crash.

"Alexander! Izzy!" Thelma cried in relief.

"Help!" Alexander grunted as he reached out to Izzy for the rope. All three of them descended on Understone as he writhed and kicked to be free of them. Izzy was the one who finally secured both of his hands behind his back with a thick knot. They then dragged him over to the wall and propped him up into a seated position.

"Izzy!" Thelma gasped. "You're OK! You found us!"

Izzy was out of breath too. Her hair was matted with mud and sweat, and she pushed it out of her face.

"I have a feeling we have this guy to thank for the episode in the river." She glared at him, and he glared back—the hint of a smile on his face.

"I'm just glad you are alive," said Thelma.

"I'm an excellent swimmer," she said, grinning.

"How long were you guys outside the window," Thelma asked. "You hear all that?"

"Uh-huh, most of it. But we've got to get out of here. Now," said Alexander.

He rushed over to Henry Bee, still dazed and limp, and grabbed him around the ribcage with one arm, helping him off the ground. Thelma was impressed. She had no idea Alexander was so strong. Thelma grabbed Annabelle's jewelry box, and then she, Izzy, Alexander, and Henry Bee began moved toward the door with urgency in their steps. Thelma was tempted to look back at Mr. Understone, but she thought better of it.

"See you never," she thought. "And good riddance."

Izzy stood in front of the door.

"Guys," she said with a quiver in her voice.

"C'mon Izzy, let's go!" Alexander was definitely impatient to escape—Henry Bee did not look good at all, hanging limply off Alexander's shoulder. They'd need to get back to the road and get him to a doctor right away.

"The door is stuck." Izzy turned around.

Thelma sighed heavily and walked to the door. She pulled. Hard. Nothing. Her eyes went immediately to the window, which was still half-open. Perhaps that was the only way out now. She was mentally calculating how they would squeeze her dad's body through the smallish space when suddenly—slam. It shut.

Understone's voice was level, perhaps even a little cheerful, as he brushed the soot off of his jacket and stood up in front of the empty hearth, rope disintegrating at his feet.

"Oh dear, I do … well, I've hardly ever had any fun these past few centuries," he said with a chilling giggle. "You little rats are a very good time indeed."

Understone raised his arm and in a split second Alexander, Izzy, and Thelma's dad levitated and flew to the middle of the room, all their toes a few inches off of the floor. Understone whacked Alexander's leg with his cane so hard that the boy yelped.

"Let them go," said Thelma through clenched teeth. "You don't need them for anything, so just let them go."

"That's a very interesting idea, little witch," said Understone. Thelma's skin prickled. "However, after careful consideration, I've decided to kill them." His ice pick gaze bored a hole through Thelma's heart and she stood helplessly. Understone laughed and made a casually dismissive motion toward Thelma. The invisible force of the motion hit her like a punch and threw her down to the ground. Her backpack opened, spilling its contents all over the floor. Twine, crumpled granola bar wrappers, and her notebook skidded to a stop in front of Alexander.

The notebook had flipped open, and Alexander's

gaze fixed on the open page, illuminated by moonlight. The notebook had opened to the vanilla orchid experiment. The sketch Thelma had drawn earlier today looked like a dim scribble in the weird light, but at the top of the page there was the question written in clear letters:

Can cultural or outside forces have an effect on how a living thing grows?

Alexander looked up from the page with the intensity of a new idea in his eyes. He made a choked noise to clear his throat.

"Mr. Understone—Zachariah, hon ... olli þér ástarharmi."

Understone froze. His expression relaxed almost imperceptibly and he turned to the suspended boy.

Alexander continued, "Sorgir slíkar átu ok hjartat mitt."

"Sveinn, hvat veiztu?" Understone spat the last word, but his eyes betrayed a softening. Thelma couldn't believe it. Alexander was talking to Understone in his language, in Old Norse. Alexander blinked hard, trying to concentrate, trying to breathe, and trying to negotiate with an ancient villain in his native tongue.

With a small hand motion, Understone let Alexander drop to the floor and he fell with a thud. Alexander rubbed his neck and motioned to the box.

"Þú elskir hana," The words didn't come easy, but Alexander was working a miracle. Thelma sat in awe of his incredible brain.

"*Hjartat mitt er þrælkat. Vaðin at vilja emk, meðan ek lífi,*" said Understone.

Alexander stared up at Understone, desperate to find the right words—ones that might set them free.

"*En þú mátt eigi …*" he struggled then stopped mid-sentence, searching for the right words, "You can't though, you know? It's impossible. It's her heart. There's no magic that can change a heart."

Just then, there was a deep rumbling from outside. Understone, distracted by the noise, looked out the window. He hardened and sneered something at Alexander in Old Norse, flinging him back up into the air with Izzy and Henry. Alexander's tactic had failed.

The ground trembled. Something huge approached. Thelma peered out the window and caught a glimpse of it, of … her. The thing from the river was sloshing and lumbering up to the cottage. This couldn't get any worse, Thelma thought. She was going to be devoured, or torn apart. Her friends and her dad were going to be dinner for this beast. She closed her eyes tight in dread.

Then something extremely unusual began to happen. The creature began a metamorphosis. The monster's silhouette against the moonlight changed, morphing and shrinking in globby fits. Sections of pale flesh bubbled out and retracted all over the monster. Soon, the figure all but disappeared. A moment later, the door that had been sealed shut squeaked open.

Hilda Hillbrook stood in the doorway, her silver pie of a hair-do no worse for wear. Understone turned to her with a look that was more disappointed parent than evil wizard.

"You missed one, Hilda. The little Indian boy."

Alexander bristled. Not that anyone should expect a psychopathic warlock from the past to be politically correct, but that was still rude.

"I'm sorry, master," said Hilda.

"Well," continued Understone, "his mind is sharp. Should be tasty for you anyhow."

Thelma gulped.

"And the blonde girl slipped through your slimy fingers, didn't she?" he tsked.

"Yes, master, she was very nimble," she said. "I'm sorry, master."

He sighed and reached out a hand to her shoulder.

"I know you're tired; you may rest now."

"Thank you, master."

With that, Hilda Hillbrook rolled her eyes back into her head and her body melted into a translucent goo that slowly and deliberately oozed across the floor and between a crack in the floorboards.

"She's earned her sleep, poor dear," Understone said under his breath.

Thelma's mind sped, trying to put all of the puzzle pieces together. Hilda Hillbrook was … what? A mess of goo? The slave to a dark wizard? A bull? A river monster? It was all too much.

"What is she?" Thelma asked, unable to control her curiosity and wild confusion.

"Hilda is my devoted helper, my hands in this

world. And she's exhausted. I don't expect I'll be able to wake her for months, now. But that isn't your concern."

Thelma remembered something Annabelle mentioned, that townspeople told stories about Under-

stone keeping a demon woman under his floorboards. That must have been Hilda. She was just as old as Understone, but some kind of shape-shifter or something. This flew in the face of every single scientific law Thelma knew of. She had never paid close enough attention to chemistry, the science of change. If she ever got out of this alive, she had so much reading to do.

The sound of her dad coughing pulled Thelma out of her thoughts and back to reality. He looked terrible, worse now than before.

The sound drew Understone's attention back to the matter at hand as well. He gave Henry's leg a light tap and snickered. "Ah, where was I?" Understone regained his train of thought. "Yes, I'm about to kill your friends. And your daddy."

"No!"

"Well, there is always my proposed trade ..."

"What are you?" she shouted.

Understone's falsely kind face darkened like a sky turned stormy. He seemed to grow taller somehow as he rushed toward Thelma and grabbed her around the neck. His fingers felt like metal clamps on her throat, and she tried to cry out but couldn't access any air.

Understone's eyes burned like white fire. "I'm getting very tired of you, witch. You will give me that key." In that moment it occurred to Thelma that he must not be able to just take it from her. Why wouldn't he grab it off of her and be done with it? For some reason, he needed her to give it to him. That meant that she had some power, or at least the neck-lace did.

Angry foam started to form on the edges of his lips. "And when you do, Annabelle and I shall leave this disgusting world forever."

There was no time for discussion. Her dad and her friends hung in the air, helpless and terrified. She was sure that Understone would not hesitate to murder them.

"If ..." Thelma said, choking, "If I agree ..."

He let go of her throat, and she gasped. "If I agree to this, you have to let them go."

Understone smiled for a moment. "All right, yes," he said.

"Really?" asked Thelma, rubbing her neck.

"No, no, not really," he said, chuckling again. "Well, fair is fair. Perhaps I won't kill all of them if you hand it over immediately, but I do need to dispose of Daddy. He's made me so cross with all that trespassing."

Anger started to boil in her belly and Thelma's skin prickled with a fiery heat. A fever swept over her like a wave. It was the same feeling as before, when they were at Magistrate's Manse, only this time it was stronger. Hotter. It felt as though a rush of newer, fiercer blood was replacing her own. Understone pointed to a dark corner of the room, and from a leather satchel that she hadn't noticed up until that very moment, a silver dagger emerged. It had golden bull's head adorning the hilt, but it was the sharp, shining blade that caught her attention. It traveled slowly through the air, past Understone, and up to her father's chest. There it hovered.

The fever intensified inside of Thelma. It was like all the times she'd been mad or embarrassed; however, instead of being out of control, this sensation was very focused. The nervous feeling in her chest turned into something more centered. A swelling ocean wave rolled inside of her. Her cheeks flushed, as did her entire body.

She looked down at her fingers; they felt like they were burning but there was no pain. The burning spread from Thelma's fingers, to her arms, and joined with the powerful energy in her core. Her whole body, her whole soul was on fire, and she was bigger than herself and so strong. She was fire.

Thelma focused her gaze on Understone, who was about to murder her father in front of her eyes. A powerful instinct compelled her to open her arms widely. She quaked, every muscle in her body tensed, and she felt the roaring warmth all around her. The heat in her body traveled from inside, past her skin, and then to a visible shield a few inches around her body. She glared at Understone, and before she truly understood what was happening, his coat burst into flames.

This was a turn of events he clearly hadn't predicted, and it broke his concentration enough so that Henry, Alexander, and Izzy dropped to the floor along with the dagger. They scrambled to get to their feet. Thelma's eyes darted around the room, frantic. She tried to catch her breath.

As the surging heat inside her died down, she felt terribly weak—like she had just run a marathon. Those flames that set Understone's jacket on fire, that were now spreading to the rest of the cottage— they had come from her. Inside of her. Thelma's head spun and she caught her breath in snatches. The opal around her neck was cool and she held onto it tightly, not knowing exactly what she had done, or for that matter, what she was.

She caught Alexander's gaze briefly before the three hostages ran out of the now-burning cottage, and she saw something strange in his eyes. He didn't know who she was anymore, either.

Understone, engulfed in flames, made screeching noises of pain. He flailed and rolled on the floor like an animal. Thelma followed the others through the door.

When they all met up outside, Izzy held Anna- belle's jewelry box and Dad leaned heavily on Alexan- der, whose brow had never been quite so furrowed. He squinted as he surveyed the marshy area.

"Guys," stammered Thelma, "I don't know what …"

"The forest," Alexander interrupted. "We have got to get back to the forest, fast."

"OK, OK." Thelma nodded, "Anywhere. I want to get as far away from here as possible."

Izzy laughed.

"What?" asked Alexander.

Something was not right. Izzy continued to chuckle deeply, too deeply. It wasn't Izzy's own laugh,

but that of Understone. When Izzy smiled, her lips revealed long yellow teeth.

Thelma and Alexander looked at each other frantically, but this time Understone did not mince words or prolong the action. Understone's voice came out of Izzy's mouth when she spoke.

"I'm pleasantly surprised. You're more powerful than I imagined." She grinned widely. "Powerful, but not very obedient. Your behavior is unsatisfactory. You'll need to spend some time with great aunt Annabelle, I think, to temper your spirit. Perhaps after some quiet reflection you will feel more cooperative."

"Izzy!" Alexander cried. "Izzy, fight him!"

Thelma paced backwards. She felt exhausted, defeated. And now she was cornered. Izzy held out the box and glared into Thelma's eyes as she turned the key and opened it up.

Thelma stared at the face of her friend, but it was twisted and possessed by darkness. Thelma felt the wind pick up strength, and the world turned into sand flying around her just as it did before. So this is how it would end. Trapped in an eternal prison. She looked to Alexander and her father and could sense that they were looking back at her, saying goodbye. She wished at least that her mother were there so she could see her face one more time.

The world was a storm of flying particles all around her. Antigravity had won. Everything began to collapse and fade. Thelma tried to call out to her dad and Alexander and tell them one last time, but she couldn't find her voice. "I love you," she thought.

Thelma heard her mother's voice echo in her ears and relished the hallucination. It seemed like it had been forever since she'd heard that comforting sound and she missed that voice so much. Then, through the fading and shifting shapes of the marsh—she saw her mother's face. It was impossible, of course. Mom was a thousand miles away.

Slowly, though, Thelma realized that this was more than a wishful fantasy. She could see her mother. Mary Bee's shape grew clear, more concrete than anything else around her. And the volume of her voice got louder—it cut unmistakably through the confusion. Thelma reached out to her, a sob stuck in her throat. Her mother was speaking to her, or to someone, but Thelma couldn't quite make out the words. Her tone was low, steady, and loud like a chant.

Mary Bee moved closer, and Thelma tried to reach out to grab onto her. Suddenly, from the darkness, there was another voice. Thelma whipped around and saw Annabelle standing on her other side. She was thin and gray as the landscape of her prison, but her expression shone with a revitalized fierceness. Thelma tried to touch her mother, but Annabelle was grabbing for Thelma too. Thelma was afraid that if she took Annabelle's hand, she would be dragged back into the prison once and for all. She shook her head with confusion, but Annabelle smiled and spoke.

Her voice was faint, but Thelma heard her say, "Take both hands."

She felt the warm grasp of her mother's hand to her right, so she extended her arm to Annabelle on her left. The moment this chain was formed, Thelma's mind spun, and in a split second the gray disappeared and she was in the present again.

The world wasn't sandy and fading anymore. In fact, everything appeared sharp and incredibly clear. The transition wasn't jarring, but completely natural. Thelma saw leaves on the trees in minute detail, the bugs and spiders of the evening populating nooks in the trees. Even through the dark, it was as clear as if she were looking through a powerful telescope. Birds, lizards, raccoon—she could see everything perfectly. It was crisp and new. Like she was in a military control center looking at satellite images of the world around her.

And then she could see that there were things beyond. Thelma squinted and perceived depths, almost like pathways in the trees, and in the sky. She knew in that moment that they were doorways, routes to other places, other worlds, maybe even other times. She was seeing everything. Knowing everything. This kind of revelation should have been shocking, or even upsetting. But in that moment, linked to her mother and Annabelle, everything was exactly predictable, exactly right, just as it was meant to be.

A great warm light washed over her, and as it did, Thelma was flooded with memories, some familiar, but some entirely foreign. She saw one vivid flash of the trip she took with her mom and dad to the Grand Canyon. But then there was a shift. She saw a small girl in very old-fashioned clothes with long golden hair, and felt so much love for this girl that it almost knocked her off her feet. "Margaret," she thought. She instinctively knew that this was Annabelle's sister, her sextuple-great-grandmother.

Another shift. Thelma was in a steamy jungle, thick with vegetation, cutting through vines with a long machete. A gorgeous black lynx walked in front of her, brushing against her legs. It looked right up at her with what could only be described as an understanding gaze.

These memories were full and vivid complete with every sensory detail. They were emotional and so personal that she knew they must, in some way, be her own.

Annabelle, Thelma, and Mary made a strong chain. Thelma looked over to her mother, but Mary's eyes were fixed on Izzy and she was still repeating those low, deliberate tones. It took Thelma a moment to realize that she too was chanting in unison with her mother and Annabelle. The words were strange and foreign to Thelma, but when she looked over at poor Izzy, who was being used as a puppet for Understone's purposes, the words seemed to be having quite an effect on her. Him. Them.

Izzy's face contorted, her features shifting from feminine to masculine to something else entirely.

Almost like a Halloween mask, but more real, more terrifying. Understone's voice bellowed out of the small girl's mouth in a scream that toed the line between utter desperation and excruciating pain. Finally, the features on Izzy's face began to swim into a bizarre-looking stew. They continued chanting, and he continued screaming.

Izzy's body fell limp on the ground as a swarm of black particles rushed from her eyes, nose, and mouth and formed a large cloud in the night air. The women, Thelma included, held steady, over and over again repeating the strange words.

Then, in a stroke of brilliance, Alexander grabbed the fallen jewelry box from the ground and held it up toward the angry black swarm. They swirled and resisted, but the pull of the box was too strong. Alexander grunted and squinted in the struggle but kept his arms strong. The particles seemed to get sucked into the small antique like a vacuum. Some tried to attack Alexander's arms and face, but all were eventually captured. Understone's creation would now be his prison. Alexander locked the box, panting. They were safe.

Mom and Annabelle released their grip on Thelma's hands, and she fell to the ground with a very unmagical thump. In the cool night air, Annabelle glowed like a living marble statue, shining and white. She bent down and touched Thelma's cheek.

"Thank you, sister. I told you that you were strong.

We can bend worlds," she said. Looking up at the sky, she sighed. "The moon is glorious this evening."

With a warm smile, she turned and walked toward the forest. As she stepped away, her form dematerialized into glittering mist and disappeared. She was free. Thelma wondered where she would go from here. Somewhere happy, she hoped, with sunlight.

Thelma rubbed both of her eyes with the palms of her hands, blinked, and looked around her. Alexander, arms cut and stung by Understone's last attack, was once again helping her dad to his feet. Izzy was rubbing her shoulder and looking utterly confused. Thelma took stock of her own physical state—bumped, bruised, but nothing broken, and all limbs accounted for.

Mary Bee walked toward the still-burning cabin, and Thelma noticed just in time to call out to her. "Mom, be careful!" Her words trailed off as she observed her mother come to edge of the flames, bend down and touch the marshy earth with her hands. The fire was extinguished. Immediately.

Analysis of Evidence

(PARTIAL)

By the following morning, Henry Bee was safe, home, and his cheerful self. Thelma doubted that he had undergone a strictly medical recovery. It was obvious that her mother's abilities were not just deductive or scientific in nature. But, Thelma realized, neither were hers.

From her seat in the living room chair, Thelma heard her dad on the kitchen telephone, sounding upbeat and occasionally laughing. He walked into the living room and took a seat on the couch opposite Thelma, next to Mom.

"Well, the good news is, Eugene is feeling fine. They're releasing him from the hospital right now, as a matter of fact. He's one lucky guy."

Thelma exhaled and fell back against the cushions, flooded with relief. In just the past twenty-four hours she had managed to put all of the people she cared most about in the whole world in life-threatening danger. If something really bad had happened to Eugene, she would never have been able to forgive herself. She took a deep breath.

"So, Thelma," Dad began.

"I ... maybe I should, sweetheart—" Mom interjected. She looked a little nervous.

Thelma stiffened a little bit. She did not want to be angry with her mom. It was a very uncomfortable feeling for her. But there were most definitely some answers Thelma wanted that only Mary Bee could provide. For starters, how on earth did she get to the Understone property right in the nick of time? Also, what kind of language did she speak that Thelma had never heard before? And that wasn't even addressing the whole issue of her putting out a house fire with her hands.

"Thelma, I know you're confused and there are a lot of things that I need to explain to you. This will sound strange, but we are special."

"OK. I got that part, Mom. I need details."

Mary continued, "Well, the name for people like us, for the women in our family, is Disiri. But we've been called lots of things throughout history."

"What does that even mean? Understone said that we were glorified hags. Are we a witch family?"

Mary scoffed a little, obviously offended by the implication. "Understone is a cockroach ... was a cockroach. That's how he got his name I imagine. Our blood is ancient, sweetheart—truly ancient." There was a glow in her blue eyes and she grabbed Thelma's hand with a squeeze.

"This isn't the way I wanted you to find out about this—because it's a beautiful thing to be what we are," she continued, focusing on each word. "Our ancestors come from the time even before pagan gods, but it was the pagan people of northern Europe gave us a name."

"The Disir?" Thelma asked.

"Yes. I passed that blood down to you just as my mother passed it down to me. Annabelle too. We aren't witches, even though there have been times where we've been persecuted as such. That's a really terrible simplification. Our power comes from the earth and from the world and from each other."

It all sounded very nice, but Thelma was frustrated. She wanted some facts. Something concrete.

"I'm having a hard time understanding this, Mom."

Mary Bee looked out the window for a moment and back at Thelma. "An example. Documented cause and effect: When Annabelle was kidnapped by Understone, ripped from the world so unnaturally—the seasons in the northern hemisphere experienced disruption."

Thelma remembered what Alexander had found in his research about 1816—the year with no summer.

"Seriously? That was because of Annabelle?" asked Thelma.

"Yes. We are … important. Our bloodline has survived since the beginning of humanity."

"You knew about Annabelle," Thelma frowned.

"Your grandmother had told me of our lost sister, but no one knew where she was—until she found you."

Thelma thought about Annabelle and felt a visceral relief that she was free. But she couldn't escape the thought of how her "sister Disiri" almost had Thelma's friends killed. There was something reckless about this power that they shared. Mom seemed pretty convinced it was this great, amazing thing, but Thelma could feel a cold danger lurking. The Disir's power wasn't simply some kind of extended motherly love. Thelma had seen firsthand that it had the capability to kidnap, to endanger, and to hurt. And it was inside her.

"OK. Ancient blood. Inside me," Thelma shook the thought away and breathed deeply. She touched the barely visible blue lines on the back of her hand. Looked like regular old dorsal metacarpal veins.

"Dad, not you too?" she asked.

"Oh, geez, no, Thel. Just your mom and you."

She could have guessed that, but at the moment was making absolutely no assumptions about anything. If her parents had told her that Mrs. Edelstein was a werewolf and Thelma's science teacher a high-functioning zombie, she wouldn't have been 100 percent surprised.

Thelma turned to her dad again, this time looking for an explanation. "You knew about this," she said. She felt betrayed and she needed data. Something that would help her quantify this whole experience.

She couldn't stop thinking about the way that Alexander looked at her last night, and it didn't feel good.

"Thelma," Mom began, "I have to apologize to you. I'm really sorry. I didn't tell you before because, honestly, I wasn't sure if you would even become one of us. Sometimes girls don't. And I never experienced any of my transformations until I was sixteen. I thought at the very least you'd have a few more years of just being a normal girl."

That had to be a joke. A normal girl? Thelma already felt like just about the least normal girl in school, and now this.

Thelma drew her knees up onto the big chair she was sitting in and pursed her lips. "What happened last night, Mom? What's going to happen to me?"

"When we grabbed hands, you, Annabelle, and I ... what did that feel like to you?"

Thelma shifted in her chair and thought.

"It felt strong. Like we had power that was really big."

Mary smiled. "Yes. You felt the power of the Disir. The energy that runs through you and me, Thelma—it is so big and strong. You will find that you are able to do so much that you never imagined you could do."

"There were memories too, though, weird flashes. But it was more than imagination—it was really real."

"Yes! Our collective memory. You were seeing through Annabelle's mind's eye and mine too. Did you see the lynx? The big cat in the jungle?"

"Yes! How did you know that?"

"That was my memory. I sent it to you. That day in the jungle was the day I found out that I was going to have a little girl."

"How?"

"The lynx told me," she said, grinning, a twinkle in her eye.

"Wait a second. Mom, you can talk to animals?"

Mary and Henry shared a smiling look. Thelma face planted dramatically on the chair. "You can talk to animals. Oh, I just give up," she sighed into a cushion.

Mom laughed lightly, "It's all right, Thelma, we'll explain everything. No more secrets. So, yes, I can communicate with animals. It can be distracting sometimes, but it is one of my gifts, and I am grateful. It helps an awful lot in my work."

Thelma thought back to all of the expeditions her mom had been on through the years—the penguins in Antarctica, the mountain lions in Japan, now the Mega-deer—communicating with animals would most definitely be a useful trick.

"Am I going to be able to communicate with animals?" she asked, sitting up.

"I don't know," said Mary. "This is where it gets a little tricky."

In Thelma's estimation, "tricky" had already shown up a long time ago.

"You'll find your gifts, or they'll find you, I suppose, and then hopefully you can use them to help people. Each one of us is unique. We're all tied together by our core, our power, but how that power manifests itself is entirely particular to the person."

Henry interjected, "That's why we need to be careful."

"What do you mean?"

"Thelma, you're only eleven years old, and … that fire …" Henry removed his glasses and rubbed his eyes.

"I've never seen anything like that before, sweetheart," Mary said.

Thelma's stomach churned. Her emotions, and her temper. Last night when Understone was just about to murder her father, she had no control. She knew that she caused the fire, but she didn't know how. It just happened.

"I don't know how I did it, Mom. It just … I got hot, and Understone was just about to—"

"Kid!" Henry put one hand on Thelma's knee and shook her good-naturedly. "You don't have to apologize! Good lord, I'm glad that you set that fire. I would have been dead meat otherwise!"

"Don't be sorry. You saved Dad's life," Mom said in a very serious tone, "I can't ever thank you enough for doing that." Her expression filled with pride. "You were brave. So brave. I don't know how you found all that courage, but we're all very lucky that you did."

Thelma felt the familiar lump in her throat and tears welled up in her eyes. Maybe it was because she was tired, or there had just been too much self-discovery and death-dodging for one long weekend.

"You've got an awful lot of power," Mom continued. "Much more than I did when I was younger. We just need to make sure that you know how to use it. How to harness it so that—"

"So that I don't burn the cafeteria down by mistake if they're serving tater tots?"

Dad laughed, "Yeah, for example."

"Self-control," Thelma said.

"Self-control," Mary echoed.

Self-control. Annabelle's words echoed in Thelma's memory: "My energy, my rage, it all became confused. I lost control."

"What about this?" Thelma held her opal necklace, "Is it a key? If so, what does it open?"

"It's a key of sorts," Mom said. "Every Disiri is given a gift from her mother, or aunt, grandmother, and it's very special. Inside that necklace, I put all of my love and prayers for you. All of my wishes."

"Like, a spell?" asked Thelma.

"I guess, maybe it's a little like a spell," conceded Mom, as she smiled and touched her shiny red hair. Then, as if she suddenly remembered something, she rolled up one of her sleeves to show a silver clasp bracelet that fit on her wrist. "This is mine, given to me by my mother. It carries all of her love for me and connects us even though she is gone now."

"But if it's a key, what does it open?"

"There's more out there than just the world you can see with your eyes, Thelma. You'll find out in time," she said.

A happy idea occurred to her. "So does this mean that I get to go to some kind of special school?" she asked.

Mary and Henry both shook their heads, amused.

"Riverfish Public is going to have to accommodate my extraordinary daughter, unfortunately," Mom said.

Henry stood up and kissed Thelma on the forehead.

"I've got the best girls in the world," he said. Thelma usually rolled her eyes when Dad got sentimental, but not today.

"I love you so much," she said.

"I love you too," he smiled.

He headed back into the kitchen to flip the apple turnovers he was baking. The house was starting to fill up with delicious warm, sweet smells.

Mom leaned toward Thelma. "Honey, there is one more thing."

Thelma furrowed her brow. She'd had just about enough excitement. She felt ready for an apple turnover and maybe some pumpkin ice cream. The Applekin Festival was underway in the town center, and her appetite was primed and ready.

"Understone," Mary began. "He was … a …"

"A what?"

"A lower demon, probably banished to earth and doomed to roam on this plane for eternity. Unless he can find a way out."

"Mom … there are just … so many things in that last sentence that I don't understand."

"There are more like him, Thelma, and they will seek you out," she touched her daughter's necklace. There is a lot of good you can do with your power, and we don't even know the start of it yet … but there are those who are going to try to hurt you. And you have to protect yourself and always be aware."

"Of, like, demons?"

"Among other things."

Thelma sighed heavily and fell back onto the chair.

"I wish this was all easy," said Mom, "but it's not. And I will always try to watch over you."

The word "try" stuck in Thelma's mind. Mom kissed her forehead and squeezed her shoulder before following Henry into the kitchen. Thelma's appetite for an apple turnover was somewhat diminished.

In her room, Thelma stared into her mirror, searching for changes. Eyes looked the same blue. Same barely managed disaster hair. Chewed-up fingernails, check. In some part of her brain, she hoped that maybe there would be some kind of outward metamorphosis, like in one of those TV shows where a normal-looking girl leaves school in June looking one way, and over summer vacation she turns into a woman. And then come September everyone's like, "Va-va-voom!" Or something like that. Only instead of instant woman-form, Thelma wouldn't have said no to some crazy laser eyes or lightning fingernails. Something cool. But nothing. She was same old Thelma, only inside, she knew something had changed completely, and there was no going back.

She examined her palms. They were cool now, but she remembered the power she had felt the previous night, and the fire. She had no roadmap, just a key. She was going to have to figure all this Disiri stuff out as it happened. Mom had said it was different for everybody, but both of her parents were seriously unnerved by the fire incident, that much was clear.

Thelma wanted to see Alexander—to talk to him about what had happened at Understone's place. She felt like she had to make sure that they were still best friends, same as ever.

Resolution

(ACCORDING TO T, IN WHICH THERE ARE PASTRIES)

Sunshine, a crisp cool breeze, and best of all—there was the mingling smells of apple and pumpkin pies in the air in the Riverfish town center. Also, Barney Bean's Cinnamon Pumpkin Chai, and Maddy Madox's world-famous Applekin fried dough. Riverfish's Applekin Festival was the best possible cure for any mood, even the "turns out I'm walking demon bait" blues.

Mom was finishing some of her research notes back at the house, so Henry and Thelma walked down to the festival carrying trays of still-hot apple turnovers for Mrs. Edelstein's booth. Everyone brought something to the festival, whether it was a talent, raffle items, or just some pie.

The Riverfish town center was decorated with orange and red paper lanterns. The streets and sidewalks buzzed with the happy chatter of people from all over the valley and beyond. Mrs. Edelstein was in her glory, handing out little cups of pumpkin crumble custard at a stand outside Arnie's Shoe Shoppe, and Ms. Oaks wore a long curly wig and gazed seriously into a crystal ball telling fortunes for a dollar. She could be heard advising every kid who sat down that they needed to work hard in school and exercise—not exactly chilling prophecy, but it was a cute act.

There was a dunk tank sponsored by the Riverfish Middle School lacrosse team, a bike raffle, and, most importantly, the jack-o-lantern carving tables that extended all the way down Main Street. These were swarming with little kids, parents, grandmas and grandpas, and even the occasional teenager.

Thelma almost dropped her tray when she saw Eugene rolling past the haunted house in a wheelchair, pushed by Ricky. Menkin was there too, wearing a sandwich board that read "RIVERFISH VALLEY PARANORMAL SOCIETY: Investigating Riverfish Valley since 1999!"

"Eugene!" Thelma ran toward him but stopped just shy of throwing her arms around his neck for fear he was still sore and hurt.

"Hello, Miss Bean," he said, smiling. "Yes, before you go crazy, I'm fine. A little bit woozy still, but the doctors said that was normal, and you know I was not about to miss the festival."

"Eugene, I'm so sorry for … for everything." Thelma bit her lip. Ricky, Menkin, and Eugene had tried so

hard to help her, but they still had no idea what had transpired at Understone's place.

"Girl, how are you going to blame yourself for some crazy animal hitting my car? I am sorry to you," he said, turning around to Ricky and Menkin. "And both of you—I didn't see it coming—"

"No one did," Menkin chirped. Her expression was so sincere, and her sandwich board was so ridiculous-looking that Thelma had to try hard not to laugh.

Ricky smiled. "We're really glad your dad's back. How …?"

"He just, um, popped out. We found the property and opened the box, and that was it!"

Thelma's voice went up about an octave—she did a terrible job of lying to people she actually cared about. Maybe someday she could share the whole story, but for now, she just wanted everyone to forget about all the creepy, scary, truly unbelievable stuff that had happened in the last few days and eat some pumpkin ice cream.

Eugene cocked his head to the side. She was not fooling him. But then after a pause, he just smiled and nodded.

"I don't suppose Mr. Bee was well enough today to bake some of his delicious apple turnovers, was he?" he asked.

"He sure was." Thelma said as she pointed to one of the many dessert tables, "*Es por alli por Senora Edelstein*," she smiled meekly and accepted an enthusiastic high five from her wheelchair-bound friend.

"That's my girl! *Excelente!*" Eugene exclaimed, and the three rolled away. Menkin turned, and Thelma could have sworn she winked at her. Could she somehow know? No. Impossible.

Thelma closed her eyes and took in the sunlight. It was so good to be home and to be safe. Some of the old men from the senior center formed a barbershop quartet in front of the church and were singing an old song about a choo-choo train. Thelma wondered why no one wrote songs about choo-choo trains anymore. She wondered whether some future barbershop quartet would write songs about high-speed rails ... or hoverboards ... space cars ... quantum teleportation ... Either way, a simple choo-choo train song was refreshing.

"Hey!" Izzy almost bowled Thelma over with a huge bear hug.

"Whoa! Hey!" Thelma steadied herself. Alexander was standing right next to Izzy. Had they come together? Thelma reminded herself that it didn't matter. She was happy to see both of them.

Izzy lowered her voice to almost a whisper. "Thelma Bee, last night was the most amazing time of my life. Honestly. I've seen some crazy stuff, I told you that, but nothing, and I mean nothing, compares to the time we had!"

Thelma was confused. "OK ... I mean, it was pretty dangerous ..." She tried to catch Alexander's eye, but he was looking off into the distance. "I really actually wanted to apologize to you ... to both of you."

"Are you serious? Thelma, you were amazing. Totally amazing. That river monster? For real? I just … I can't believe we had no camera. None of it was documented. I still have to debrief Ricky and what's-her-face …"

"Menkin," Alexander said, still looking far away.

"Right. Whatever. I'm still compiling my notes."

"Don't! Um … I mean. I think we should wait on telling anybody anything. I—"

Alexander finally looked at Thelma and caught her panicked look. "I think what Thelma's trying to say is that there's a lot more research that needs to be done before we submit anything formal. Also, Thelma's mom is involved in a lot of really top-secret fieldwork, so we can't put that in jeopardy," he said.

Izzy held her braid in one hand and furrowed her brow. "Yeah. OK, I guess that makes sense. So, classified. For now."

Thelma exhaled in relief. "Yeah. Classified for now. That's good. Hey, Izzy, I have a school question for Alexander. Could …"

"No! So boring! Ugh, fine, I'm going to go and try to dunk one of those lacrosse team weirdoes," said Izzy as she strutted away, braid swinging behind her like a cat's tail.

Alexander and Thelma stood in the middle of the bustling street. She didn't know how to start.

"Hey," she said.

"Hey." He looked sheepish.

"Are you mad at me?"

"No." He removed his glasses, now held together with conspicuous beige tape, and cleaned them with the bottom of his sweater. "I'm not mad, Thelma. Why would I be mad? I mean you basically saved our lives."

"You did too!"

"No. I tried and failed. You ... you exploded."

Thelma felt her face get warm. She knew it—this was going to change everything. They'd always been on the same page, on the same team. Now she was something different. She started to well up a little, but kept her tears in check.

"I couldn't help it, Alexander. I'm sorry if I'm a freak and you hate me now." In that moment she hated being what she was. All she wanted was for everything with Alexander to stay exactly the same, even though she knew it was impossible. She felt kind of sick, not even in the mood for ice cream anymore.

She was taken completely off guard when Alexander grabbed her by the shoulders and pulled her into a hug. He held her so tight she almost couldn't breathe, but it felt good. And he smelled like nice shampoo, probably Lana's.

When he finally let her go, it was Alexander who had tears in his eyes.

"Thelma Bee, are you crazy? A freak? You're ... you're magical. Like, literally magical. I was just scared. I had never seen you like that before, and I was afraid."

"Afraid of me?"

"No. Afraid that you were ... that I was going to

lose you." He paused, a little embarrassed. "I mean, you're my best friend." Thelma felt the whole world click back into place.

She stared up at Alexander and asked a question she'd pondered since the previous night.

"What did you say to him?" she asked

"Huh?"

"Understone, when you talked to him in Norse … which was incredible, by the way …"

He scratched the back of his head and squinted.

"Um, I just said that I understood that he felt, like, broken because the person he loved didn't love him back. And that I was sorry because that stinks. But that you can't make someone … you know, like you a certain way if they don't."

Thelma nodded, feeling a little embarrassed, though she didn't really understand why.

"Oh," she said, "Super smart. It was a good strategy."

"Yeah," he said. "Worked for a minute at least."

"Dunked!" Izzy's triumphant voice rang out from across the street among laughs and cheers. Thelma looked over and saw that her friend had indeed successfully sent the newest member of the lacrosse team into a vat of water. Jenny Sullivan was soaking wet as she emerged, mascara dripping in gray lines down her face. All her seventh- and eighth-grade teammates were laughing good naturedly, so she forced a fake smile through her obvious fury. It was the best Applekin Festival in the history of mankind.

Thelma smiled and slid her arm through Alexander's like they were a gentleman and a lady from some far-off time period. The barbershop quartet kept on singing about that choo-choo train as Thelma Bee and Alexander Oldtree weaved their way through the busy festival crowd to get themselves some Applekin fried dough.

As the sun set over Riverfish, they began to light the jack-o-lanterns. Izzy joined Alexander and Thelma as they stood by the river's edge and watched the water illuminate with hundreds of orange, ghoulish

faces. 100 percent, Thelma thought. Appreciate this moment 100 percent.

Just a few blocks away at Bee's Very Unusual Antiques, a silent figure slipped through the back door and unlocked Henry's safe. The figure grabbed a small antique jewelry box and slipped it into its coat pocket. As the figure escaped down a narrow River-fish alley, it spied a small girl with a messy ponytail standing arm in arm with two other children, looking out over the river.

Hilda Hillbrook's eyes flashed red, and she studied the girl for many moments before flicking a long silver tongue behind her teeth, twitching her nose, and slipping out of sight. Inside the jewelry box, Mr. Understone gave a long, quiet laugh.

The Scientific Method

It was dark when Thelma and Henry returned to their home on Maple Avenue with bellies full of all the delicious treats Riverfish had to offer. It had been an excellent year for the pumpkin crumble, and Thelma had indulged happily.

She peered out the window of her room onto the peaceful river and the backyard garden. In the silvery moonlight, something unexpected was brightly illuminated. The sprouting white petal of a vanilla orchid.

Thelma raised her hands to her head in disbelief. The vanilla orchid had grown from a tiny cutting to a long, winding vine in just days. She was momentarily thrilled—the experiment had worked! But she quickly sobered and got out her notebook.

Thelma sighed and bit her lower lip in contemplation. The plant could not have grown at this rate naturally. It was impossible. But impossible or not, it did happen—so she would document every detail. That's what scientists do.

She flipped back and forth between her lists. There was a lot of data to organize, not that she knew where to begin. She turned to the page that she had begun at Barney Beans just a few days ago, though it seemed like a million years.

What happens on the other side?

Technically, she had collected a ton of information on this. Her Ghost Facts list trailed onto three pages. But as to that question—she still couldn't formulate a conclusion. She pictured Annabelle though, beautiful and glittering—disappearing into the trees. Where was she going? What happens on the other side? It would remain an investigation in progress.

She flipped back to the vanilla orchid experiment and took a deep breath, putting her pen to the notebook paper.

Day 7: Experimental orchid is GROWING at an alarming rate. It has nearly overtaken the supports. Although it is tempting to consider this a confirmation of my hypothesis, recent developments regarding . . .

She paused and bit the end of her pen, then continued writing.

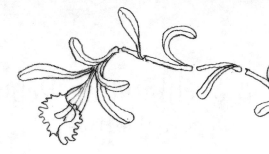

... regarding certain unscientific events have occurred. We will need to replicate the results before any definitive conclusion can be drawn. Tomorrow we begin again. Expectations remain <u>HIGH</u>!

She underlined that last bit twice.

A Spellbinding Debut from Erin Petti

Erin Petti lives by the ocean in Massachusetts and loves to read about magic, dinosaurs, folklore, and ghosts. She has a masters in education and a background in improvisational comedy. Erin lives with her husband, excellent toddler, and cat (who she suspects likes her better than she's letting on). Follow Erin at www.erinpetti.com or @empetti

FANTASY & MAGIC / PARANORMAL / JUVENILE FICTION

Ghost-story lover and debut author ERIN PETTI
has written a quirky story for fans of *The Goonies*, *Goosebumps*, and *Coraline*.

Eleven-year-old budding scientist Thelma Bee has adventure in her blood. But she gets more than she bargained for when a ghost kidnaps her father. Now her only clues are a strange jewelry box and the word "Return," whispered to her by the ghost. It's up to Thelma to get her dad back, and it might be more dangerous than she thought—there's someone wielding dark magic, and they're coming after her next.

ADVANCED READING COPY—NOT FOR SALE

Pub date: September 6, 2016
ISBN: 978-1-938063-72-5 | 978-1-938063-73-2 (ebook)

Trade cloth | 5.5" × 8" | 216 pages | $16.99

Distributed by PGW/Perseus
orderentry@perseusbooks.com

Before quoting for review, please consult the
final edition or check with the publisher.

Full e-galley available upon request.
Contact sammy@mightymedia.com

mighty media JUNIOR READERS

mightymediapress.com